THE LAWYER

STAY OF EXECUTION

as written by
WAYNE D. DUNDEE

AN EDWARD A. GRAINGER SERIES

ISBN: 978-0-9905916-8-9

 BEAT to a PULP
PO Box 173
Freeville, New York 13068
USA
Email: btapzine@beattoapulp.com
Visit us at www.beattoapulp.com

CONTENTS

    by Edward A. Grainger

CHAPTER ONE

If he hadn't heard the sound of gunshots coming from the direction of the hardscrabble little farm, The Lawyer would have ridden wide of the place and never given it a second thought. But the gunfire changed everything. It wouldn't allow him to ride around. Not when he knew Crenshaw was running only a short distance out ahead of him; not when he knew all too well the man's propensity for violence. Where there was shooting and Lou Crenshaw was in close proximity, only a fool would figure he wasn't somehow mixed up in it.

The Lawyer stopped his horse on the crest of a long slope, concealed by thick foliage stained with riotous fall coloring. He held a spyglass to his right eye, carefully studying the modest house and cluster of weathered, sun-bleached outbuildings in the clearing below.

Had anyone been studying him in return, they would have seen a man in his middle thirties, average in height, lean and solid of build. His face was evenly featured, considered handsome by most, distinguished by a well-trimmed beard of the same dark brown color as his hair, though the latter was showing signs of needing a barber. On his head rested a hat of rather curious design, its brim not quite as broad as most worn on the prairies of northeast Texas and points further west, while its blunt crown rose a good three to four inches higher than that of the popular and frequently seen flat-crowned Stetson. Additionally, the rest of the man's garb, although presently streaked with dust from many long hours on the trail, was of uncommonly good cut and quality, from his tight-fitting, soft-leather gloves to his custom boots. It would be easy to peg him as a bit of a dandy. And, although the big Remington revolver on his right hip might serve to temper this impression somewhat, there was no missing the fact that it, too, rode in a hand-tooled leather holster.

The man's name was J.D. Miller, although in more and more parts of the country he was becoming increasingly well known (some would say notorious) as The Lawyer.

In the not too distant past, Miller *had* been an attorney at law. A respected and successful one. Until the horrific, soul-scarring day when he returned home from an intense, drawn-out court session to find his entire family gruesomely slaughtered—the charred remains scarcely recognizable in the smoldering ruins of what had once been their house.

Following that, like a phoenix rising out of the ashes, The Lawyer had been born. A man still committed to upholding laws and dispensing justice—but strictly in accordance to his own interpretations and definitions. His main focus, naturally, was the rabid dogs that butchered his family. In order to finance his long, relentless search for these men, who had subsequently scattered like windblown debris, The Lawyer found it necessary to sometimes hire out for "side jobs" where the existing laws or those representing them had been corrupted or otherwise diverted from a result of true and proper justice.

The matter of Crenshaw, however was not an ancillary pursuit. The Lawyer had believed there were only three men who'd invaded his home and he had eliminated the last of those—a blacksmith who tried to deal for his life but instead ended up the late night snack for a gator in a Louisiana swamp. But later, a local rummy field hand that did the odd chore around town, a man named Bowers, had the courage to come forward to The Lawyer and let him know that he had witnessed a total of seven men ride out to the Miller farm. Bowers recognized one of them as Crenshaw, whom he ran into earlier that day when he'd been hanging around the livery stable.

The Lawyer abruptly halted scanning with the spyglass and held it fixed on a pole corral extending out from one end of a faded barn in the farm clearing below. Inside the corral were three horses—three dead horses. Two of them were heavy-chested and big-rumped, a matched pulling team; the third was smaller and sleeker, a riding mount. The lack of rigor or bloating told The Lawyer that the animals had died at nearly the same time and hadn't been dead for very long. The splashes of fresh blood and the bullet holes in the head of each told the rest. The horses had recently been gunned down, accounting for at least part of the shooting The Lawyer had heard from back up the trail.

The Lawyer swore under his breath. The fact that the saddle horse was a blaze-faced gelding his spyglass had caught fleeting glimpses of more than once in the past few days—being ridden by none other than Lou Crenshaw—gave a clear idea who was behind the killing of the animals. And from there The Lawyer quickly formed a hunch as to why.

But before he was able to ponder the subject further, faint movement elsewhere drew his attention away from the corral. At the opposite end of the barn, nearly hidden behind its corner, he now saw the forms of a man and woman he apparently had skimmed over without noticing earlier. The man lay on his back, legs splayed wide, a large scarlet oval spreading down across his stomach. The woman was slumped over him, their bodies pressed together. Only when the woman moved again did The Lawyer realize she hadn't been slumped over the body so much as leaning intently to the task of administering to the wound. As he watched, The Lawyer saw something more. The woman was very pregnant.

The Lawyer swore again. He had no choice but to go down there and try to be of assistance to the pair. However much time it cost him, he knew, would be time that Crenshaw—who obviously had struck and was now on the move again—would use to his full advantage for hopefully eluding The Lawyer altogether or, at the very least, re-widening the gap between them that had gotten so precariously narrowed.

The Lawyer also knew that, in addition to being desperate and dangerous, Crenshaw could be damned crafty. Which meant that, no matter how likely it seemed he had already ridden on from here, there remained the chance he might have stuck around to set up an ambush for his pursuer. Keeping this in mind, The Lawyer did not proceed down to the farm clearing until after he'd thoroughly scoped the layout one more time and then moved to a spot at the top of the slope where a thicker growth of brush and scattered saplings spilled down, providing cover all the way to the flat.

Having made the descent without incident, The Lawyer dismounted and led his horse over to the corner of the barn where the man and woman were still on the ground. As he drew near, the woman looked up. Somewhat surprisingly, whatever her appraisal of him concluded, it caused no fear to show on her face. In return, The Lawyer saw that she was a young woman barely into her twenties. She was average looking, though leaning a bit more toward the pretty side than the plain, with dark hair and dusky skin that suggested some Mexican blood in her. From what he could tell of the wounded man, whom he reckoned to be the young woman's husband, he was stocky in build (the type some termed "hard fat"), not more than half a dozen years older than his wife, with a shock of rust-colored hair and a ruddy complexion under a peach fuzz pelt of reddish-gold facial hair that would probably never coarsen into as thick a beard as he was trying for.

Before The Lawyer could say anything, the young woman blurted out, "My husband has been shot by a

5

villainous horse thief. I think I finally have the bleeding stopped, but he's lost a lot of blood. I fear he is in a bad way."

"A horse thief, you say?"

The woman nodded. "Yes, we were in the barn—my husband was repairing some feed bunks and I'd brought him out a cup of coffee. When we heard the horses starting to fuss in the corral, we went to check on what was wrong. There was a man there, a complete stranger, who had taken the saddle off his own horse and was getting ready to put it on one of ours."

"Not one of the plow horses laying out there now?"

"No. We also have … had … two riding horses. After he shot my husband for trying to interfere, the stranger went ahead and took them both. He rode one and led the other on a rope."

The Lawyer clenched his teeth. The hunch he'd had upon first spotting his quarry's blaze-face with a bullet through its brain was now confirmed. Crenshaw was not only on the move again but was doing so on a fresh horse—with a second one in tow that he could periodically switch to so he'd have a rested mount available at all times. And by killing his former ride as well as even the plow horses, Crenshaw assured that The Lawyer was left no recourse but to stick with his hard-ridden Morgan. Which meant that, even if he wasn't being delayed by assisting the farm couple and attempted to continue in immediate pursuit, The Lawyer would have no hope of keeping pace with Crenshaw and his set of fresh horses.

Not missing the contemplative expression on The

Lawyer's face, the young woman said, "Do you know the identity of the man I've described?"

"Unfortunately, yes. His name is Crenshaw," The Lawyer replied. "You called him villainous? That only begins to tell it. He's as dangerous and vile as anything walking on two legs."

"You're after him, aren't you?"

"Been on his trail for some time. Had it figured to catch up with him soon. I regret I wasn't able to make it before he showed up here and caused this trouble."

"You certainly can't blame yourself for that. Are you a lawman?"

"I'm working in the interest of law and justice, yes," The Lawyer answered.

"But you'll stay and help us … help my husband … Won't you?"

"Of course," The Lawyer assured her. He knelt down and motioned for the woman to move her hand so he could have a look at the injured man's wound.

"I should tell you that we're the Brandywines—I'm Eloise, this is my husband Howard." Eloise's nerves were clearly at work, making her overly talkative. "I can't tell you how grateful we are that you came along."

Because he knew she expected it in return, The Lawyer told her, "My name is Smith. J.D. Smith." He used the alias because his actual name was becoming too closely associated with the growing notoriety of The Lawyer.

Eloise held her tongue then, remaining quiet while her husband's wound was examined. The bullet had gone in half way between heart and collarbone. As best

The Lawyer could tell, it hadn't passed all the way through. But, in order to make sure, he had to lift the victim's shoulder and roll him part way over onto his side. Howard Brandywine's face was drained of color and dotted with beads of clammy sweat. He was barely clinging to consciousness yet had enough left so that when The Lawyer moved him he issued a low groan from the pain.

Having seen what he needed to, The Lawyer eased Howard onto his back once more. "The bullet didn't pass through, it's still in him," he said. "That's both good and bad. It's good because your success at stopping the bleeding at the entrance point means no more blood loss. But the bad part is that we can't leave the slug in there for very long due to risk of infection setting in. I know a little bit about gunshot wounds, but that bullet is too deep and too near the heart for me to go digging around. We need to get your husband to a doctor."

"The nearest one is at Carstaris Crossing. That's a little over twenty miles to the south," Eloise said anxiously.

"Do you have a functioning wagon or buckboard?"

"There's a wagon in that shed over there," said Eloise, pointing. "But we no longer have any animals to pull it."

"We've got my horse," The Lawyer said with a head tip toward his tall Morgan. "Redemption's never pulled a wagon before, but she's adaptable and obedient. She'll get the job done."

"She's a beauty. But she already looks pretty

tuckered out. It will be asking a lot of her to pull that heavy old wagon."

"No matter. Redemption will come through. A greater concern than how she'll hold up should be how rough the wagon trip may be on your husband ... and you." The Lawyer furled a brow somewhat uncomfortably. "Not to be indelicate or too personal, but I'm the father of two children and it looks to me like you're very nearly ready to deliver that child you're carrying."

Eloise smiled vaguely at his discomfort. "Your experience has given you a keen eye. Yes, my child is due practically any day. A local midwife, a neighbor woman by the name of Ida Lisle, was scheduled to come and stay with us until the baby arrived. But she sent word yesterday that she's unable to make it." Now Eloise's expression hardened with distaste. "Her lout of a husband got drunk and beat her. Not for the first time. But this time she's injured so badly—suffering a broken hip from being knocked down, among other things—that she can hardly get around for her own purposes, let alone assist anyone else."

"Any man who beats a woman that way is no man at all," snarled The Lawyer. "But our immediate focus has to stay on you and your husband. It sounds like both of you may have need of that doctor when we get to town."

"I feel so helpless and foolish, this being my first baby and all," Eloise lamented. "If I knew even a little bit about—"

"You can't help not knowing what you've never

had any experience at," The Lawyer cut her off. "If we get started right away, we should be able to make it to town by dusk or shortly after. What you need to decide is if you want to take the risk of moving your husband. Like I said, the wagon ride will no doubt be a little rough on both of you. In my opinion, though, it would be more of a risk to wait for the time it would take me to ride to town alone and bring the doctor back here."

"I agree," Eloise responded firmly. "By all means, I think it best we travel *to* the doctor."

The Lawyer nodded. "All right, then. Show me where that wagon is. Then, while I'm getting Redemption hooked up, you gather what you'll need for the trip. Bring something to use for bandages in case his bleeding starts again. And grab plenty of blankets—for your husband to lie on and also to wrap him in. Yourself as well. When the sun starts going down, it'll turn chilly out there on the trail. Bring some whiskey, too, if you've got it. For added warmth and to help dull his pain if need be."

CHAPTER TWO

Carstairs Crossing was a fair-sized community built at the intersection of random trails feeding in from ranches to the north and south and a more established east-west road connecting to other towns in those general directions. Full darkness had edged out the last glimmer of dusk by the time The Lawyer steered the Brandywine wagon down the main street, their trip from the farm having taken a bit longer than antici-pated. The Lawyer's prediction about how Redemption would perform at her pulling task, however, was right on the money. Once the sturdy Morgan got used to the harness and understood what was required of her, she leaned smartly into the task.

Eloise directed The Lawyer to turn down a side street where, after only a short ways, she then instructed him to pull up in front of a modest wood frame house with a rectangular extension off the back end. The Lawyer surmised this was the doctor's home and would soon learn the extension was his office and treatment room.

When the medic appeared, he introduced himself as Dr. Simes. He was a tall, lanky sort with a knobby

Adam's apple bobbing around in a long, stringy neck and iron gray hair that kept spilling from a center part down around either side of a narrow, wedge-shaped face. After a quick initial look at the wounded man's condition, he hurried back inside his office and returned with a solid, rigid stretcher upon which he and The Lawyer transported Howard Brandywine from the wagon to an examination table in the doc's treatment room.

Simes's wife and nurse—a plump, round-faced woman with snow white hair worn in a tight bun—held the door for the stretcher bearers and then scurried about making preparations and assisting with other chores. One of these was to usher Eloise and The Lawyer into the office area to wait. Before closing the door to the treatment room and disappearing on the other side of it, she assured them they would be notified as soon as there was something to report. She also pointed out a countertop hand pump if they needed something to drink and a stack of old newspapers and Monkey Wards catalogs if they wanted to help pass the time.

In the months since starting out on the trail of his family's killers, The Lawyer had learned the value of patience. Had he not, his initial wild rage and sense of urgency for immediate retribution would have driven him mad. His craving for swift revenge never lessened, but he learned to temper it and hold it in check with cold, steady determination; knowing he would stay the course and do what he'd set out to do, no matter how long it took. It was because of this that he was able to sit there and wait so calmly in a straight-backed wooden chair outside the treatment room, rather than climb the walls out of frustration for not being back on the trail of Lou Crenshaw.

Actually, he supposed, if he chose to, it would be perfectly acceptable for him to leave at any point now. After all, he'd done the charitable thing, put his own business on hold in order to help complete strangers in need. There wasn't much more he could do. From here it was all in Simes's hands. Still, he for some reason felt compelled to stick around at least long enough to hear what the doctor had to say. Plus there was the matter of the young mother-to-be. She naturally was dealing with heightened nervousness about her husband's condition. And, considering her own condition, it was probably best she wasn't left sitting alone. If The Lawyer allowed himself to be anxious about something, it would be over the possibility that too much fretting on her part might cause Eloise to go suddenly into labor.

Besides, as far as taking out after Crenshaw again, there was nothing more he could do yet tonight, regardless of anything else. It was dark, the murdering dog had gotten the jump during the daylight hours that The Lawyer had already spent with the Brandywines and, for however long Crenshaw had stayed on the move before making night camp, he would have been traveling fast and hard with his pair of fresh horses. The Lawyer's best bet was to get himself and Redemption well rested during the overnight hours, maybe pick up a spare horse of his own before heading out in the morning, and then ride like hell to once again close on his quarry.

Nearly an hour passed before Dr. Simes emerged from the treatment room, wiping his hands on a bloody towel. The sight of the towel caused Eloise's eyes to bug fearfully but then the wide, reassuring smile on the face of the doc quickly helped her relax again.

"That dirty devil of a slug was burrowed in mighty deep and did *not* want to cooperate about coming out," Simes announced. "But, finally, I won the tug of war!"

"Is Howard going to be all right?" Eloise wanted to know.

"Your husband is going to be plenty stiff and sore for a spell," Simes told her. "But all of that will pass in time, and then he'll be back fit as a fiddle. Fortunately, the bullet hit no bones or major blood vessels. It sliced up muscle tissue in a couple places, but I did some stitching to repair that. That's a big part of what will leave him sore. All and all, though—even if it doesn't seem like it, considering he got shot in the first place, and it surely won't *feel* like it to him when he first wakes up—he's a lucky man."

"Can I go in and see him?" pleaded Eloise.

Simes frowned. "He's still pretty out of it from the chloroform, I doubt he'd even know you were there. It's really best to let him rest for …" The doctor's words trailed off as he wilted under Eloise's imploring gaze. "Oh, all right. But try not to disturb him and don't plan on staying for very long."

After the girl had scurried from the room, Simes put aside his towel and went over to the counter where he pumped himself a glass of water. He took a long drink and then turned back to face The Lawyer. "I didn't want to alarm Mrs. Brandywine unduly," he said, "but that young man of hers was in mighty rough shape by the time you got him here. Before much longer there'd've been a good chance he wouldn't have made it. Even though the wound had been plugged on the outside, you see, there was still internal bleeding. It was taking a serious toll."

"We briefly debated the risk of hauling him this far in a wagon as opposed to riding in and taking you back out to him," The Lawyer admitted. "Sounds like it's a good thing we made the choice we did."

"Indeed. He'd never have lasted long enough the other way." The doctor finished draining his glass of water. "Also a mighty good thing you showed up out there the way you did to lend a hand, Mr. ... ah, Smith, was it?"

As they were getting Howard Brandywine from the wagon to the treatment room, Eloise and The Lawyer had given Simes a hurried rundown of the circumstances that led to their delivery of a man who'd been shot. As her part of that, Eloise had mentioned the name The Lawyer had given her.

Detecting the hint of sarcasm or maybe flat-out suspicion in Simes's tone as he repeated the alias, The Lawyer nevertheless responded flatly, calmly, "That's right ... Smith."

"Uh-huh. And the fella who shot Howard was a horse thief?"

"Among other things. His name is Crenshaw. Trust me, he's done considerably worse than steal horses."

"I'm taking it, from the way you showed up on his heels, that you were tracking him. But I don't see any kind of lawman's badge on you. That make you a bounty hunter?"

"That's a close enough call." The Lawyer set his jaw. "Look, Doc, I understand how bringing a man to your doorstep who's been shot is naturally going to arouse your curiosity and maybe even suspicions. But I'm going to have go through all of this all over again with your local marshal or sheriff or what have you, so why don't we send for him and I can answer whatever else needs to be answered without having to repeat myself any more than necessary."

Doc Simes grunted. "That would be a right sensible thing … *if* we had a marshal or sheriff here in Carstairs Crossing. But we don't. Things generally stay pretty quiet hereabouts so nobody's ever felt a strong enough need to go to the trouble of electing or appointing such. There's a U.S. Marshal who passes through every now and then, folks seem to think that's sufficient."

The Lawyer arched a brow. "Things are generally pretty quiet around here, eh? Yet it seemed clear that Brandywine's wasn't the first bullet hole you ever went digging into."

"It should also be clear," Simes replied evenly, "that I happen to have a few decades on me, sir. And, in case you haven't noticed in your travels, there are places outside of Carstairs Crossing where a man of medicine might spend time plying his trade and thereby might run into other bullet holes."

The Lawyer nodded. "Fair enough."

The doctor sighed as he cast a glance in the direction of the treatment room's closed door. "I guess I'd better go in there and encourage Mrs. Brandywine to let her husband get some rest."

"Probably be a good idea for her to get some herself," The Lawyer suggested. "From what she told me—and as I'm sure you've noticed—she's due to go into labor just about any time."

"Yes. Nor did that fact escape the notice of my dear wife. She's making some preparations even as we speak. We have accommodations, you see, for keeping patients overnight when necessary. Or for a few nights if need be. I'd say the Brandywines qualify."

"I agree. It's good to hear you're set up for that."

"What about you? I figure you'll be looking to spend the night in town also?"

"You figure right. For starters, that's my saddle horse hitched to the Brandywine wagon outside and I'll be wanting to get her stabled and taken good care of. She's earned it. Then I'll worry about myself."

Simes reached up and rubbed a palm back and forth on the nape of his neck. "You passed a livery stable on the way in. Back down near to the end of our main street. Run by a fella named Huffman. He'll take good care of your animal and I'm sure he'll look after the Brandywine wagon, too, until they're ready to reclaim it. As for you, sorry to say we don't have a hotel in town. There are a couple boarding houses, but they're both run by elderly widows who've likely turned in by this hour and don't really cotton to single-night boarders anyway. And the Brandywines will pretty much fill up anything I could offer you here."

The Lawyer shook his head. "No, I don't want to do anything that might disturb them more than they've already been put through."

"That leaves Jorgeson's saloon as your best bet. You'll find it catty-cornered across the street from the livery stable. Jorgeson rents out sleeping rooms and he even has a shed out back for taking baths, except when the weather's too cold. And he's usually got the makings for sandwiches if you want something to eat." The doc rubbed his neck some more before continuing. "You'll need to keep in mind the rooms can be a little noisy, of course, until the bar closes. But, this being a weeknight, I don't expect you'll find things too rowdy over there. A final thing to consider is that you can rent rooms just for sleeping or, if you're so inclined … some, er, company can be—"

"Save it. I'm not so inclined."

Simes made no comment but flashed a brief, approving smile.

Starting toward the exit, The Lawyer said over his shoulder, "Tell the Brandywines I'll stop by in the morning before I head out of town."

CHAPTER THREE

Doc Simes's directions were easy to follow, especially considering the modest size of Carstairs Crossing. Huffman, the livery stable proprietor, proved every bit as affable and accommodating as advertised and The Lawyer sensed right away that he was leaving Redemption in good hands.

Jorgeson's saloon was marked only by a long, rectangular plank leaning up against the outside wall to the right of the entrance. Someone had hand-painted the word SALOON in lopsided letters running vertically down the length of the plank. Inside, the simple motif was continued throughout the large, high-ceilinged room. Off to one side, the bar consisted of more thick planks nailed across the tops of waist high wooden barrels. In the middle of the room were four round-topped tables circled by a collection of mismatched chairs. At the far end, a narrow, doorway-lined hallway extended away from the bar area; The Lawyer reckoned the doorways opened to the sleeping—or frolicking—rooms he'd been told about.

He took a spot at the bar, shrugging his saddlebags off his shoulder and laying them on the bar top along with his Winchester. He also removed his hat and carefully placed it so that it rested on the flat of its crown beside his other gear.

The bar was otherwise unoccupied except for the bartender who was leaning on it from the other side down at the opposite end. If this was Jorgeson, he was another long, lanky number with an elongated face framed by a thick headful of pale yellow hair, bushy sideburns, and a drooping mustache bracketing a narrow mouth. The only other customers in the place were three elderly men playing cribbage at one of the tables and passing around a bottle of whiskey that they took occasional swigs from without benefit of glasses. So far, so good, The Lawyer thought; if things stayed as quiet as this, he'd have no trouble getting some sleep as soon as he occupied his room.

Putting aside the dog-eared dime novel he'd been reading, the barkeep shuffled down to where The Lawyer was and tried to put some enthusiasm in his weary smile as he said, "Evenin', mister. What can I get you?"

"A glass of beer. No matter the brand, just make it the coldest you got. And a shot of your best whiskey."

"Fix you right up."

"I could use something to eat, too."

"Have to be sandwiches. Got some cold cuts and sourdough bread in the back. Or some roast beef that could be sliced up. And maybe enough porridge left for one more bowl."

"I'll have a sandwich each of the cold cuts and beef. Save the porridge."

The barkeep nodded. "I'll get my girl started on the sandwiches, then have your drinks right up for ya."

When the drinks came, the whiskey was surprisingly good. The beer was cold, as requested, but that was about all that could be said for it.

After he'd thrown down the first slug of whiskey, The Lawyer pulled a clip of paper money from his pocket, spread some bills on the bar and tapped his glass for a refill. As it was being poured, he said, "I'm told you rent sleeping rooms. Do you have one available for tonight?"

"I do."

"Bath?"

"We always keep hot water ready in the back. It's a quarter for two pails, soap, and a clean towel. A dime extra if you want my girl to carry the pails back for you."

"I can manage my own pails," The Lawyer told him. "And that sleeping room? That's all I mean to use it for—sleeping. Alone."

"However you say, mister."

The Lawyer motioned for the man to take what payment he needed from the bills. After the barkeep had made change, a red-haired young woman came out from around one end of the partition that ran behind the bar. She was carrying a tray with two thick sandwiches on a plate.

As she moved toward The Lawyer, the girl did so in slow, measured steps, as if in pain, and she held her chin tucked down so that her long hair spilled forward on the sides, hiding much of her face. Nevertheless, The

Lawyer didn't miss the traces of deep purple bruising on one cheek and the scabbed-over split on her bottom lip. He immediately felt the heat of anger crawl up his face, at the same time remembering what Eloise Brandywine had told him about the neighbor woman who'd been abused so badly by her husband. Damn! Was the pastime of the men in this area beating up their women?

His ire surging, The Lawyer shot a hard glare in the direction of the barkeep. He jumped to a conclusion that the girl was likely one of the "companions" available for visits to the rooms in back, and it was well known how roughly some pimps and saloonkeepers treated their soiled doves. The Lawyer had always despised abuse of the young and vulnerable and, since the loss of his own wife and children, his reaction to signs of this kind of mistreatment was more explosive than ever.

Still, at least for the moment, he restrained himself from speaking up and demanding to know what had happened to the redhead. One part of him urged this, but another part—a coldly practical and perhaps somewhat selfish part—questioned the advisability of injecting himself into the misfortune of a saloon girl who was a complete stranger to him. After all, he was already involved with the Brandywines—did he really want to risk getting caught up in something else that might cost him more time before he'd be able to get back on the trail of Lou Crenshaw?

Before The Lawyer could make up his mind, the front door burst open and three gaunt-faced, work-worn wranglers made a boisterous entrance, spurs chiming and boot heels clomping loudly on the wooden floor. They strode past The Lawyer and bellied up to the bar several feet away from him. At the sight of these new arrivals, the red-haired girl thrust the tray of food down in front of The Lawyer then spun on her heel and quickly disappeared again behind the partition.

One of the wranglers let out a rip. "Whoooee!" He was somewhat younger than his two companions and carried himself with an arrogant swagger that suggested he considered himself a cut above them and probably most other folks. His clothes were dust-streaked, indicating he'd done some share of a hard day's work, but the oversized silver conches decorating the front of his black leather vest still shone brightly and more of the same comprised his hatband. The Colt riding low on his right hip, in a black leather holster that matched his vest, also had a silver overlay on the exposed metal and its pearl grips gleamed as white as strained milk. In contrast, the pair of veteran wranglers accompanying this younger specimen were clad in drab, dusty, somewhat shabby yet durable range duds minus any flashy accessories.

The flashy one slapped his palm down on the plank bar top. "Jorgeson, you ol' rotgut rustler, Johnny Hollister has showed up with money to spend and a powerful thirst to be quenched. Set up a bottle and a couple glasses for my pards here, Clancy and Mort." He jerked a thumb, indicating each of the other men in turn. "Then set up another bottle for me and don't bother with no glass."

Jorgeson grunted. "There's thirsty talk if I ever

heard it. And that's music to any saloonkeeper's ears—the sound of a thirsty man with the money to fill his need."

Johnny let out a whoop of laughter. "You hear that, boys? I think ol' Jorgeson just threw what you call a not-so-subtle hint that he'd like to see some money on top of the bar before he gets too anxious to fork over any liquor from his side."

With a sour twist to his mouth, the wrangler Johnny had indicated as Mort said, "That's Jorgeson for you. He'd pinch a penny 'til it squealed and wouldn't offer a charity drink to even the most desperate desert rat who crawled in after six months in the brain-fryin' sun."

"Well, a-course not," chimed in Clancy, the other veteran wrangler. "You can't expect Jorgeson to run his business like a charity—he's got to make money in order to maintain the upkeep on this luxurious establishment he's got goin' here." With the last, he spread his arms wide to sarcastically indicate the meager simplicity of their surroundings.

Everybody got a good laugh over that. Even Jorgeson couldn't hold back a thin, begrudging smile.

From where he sat down the bar a ways, The Lawyer tried to ignore the guffawing trio. He took a bite of the beef sandwich, finding it quite good, and thought about how much better yet it would be if things were still as peaceful as they'd been when he first came in.

"But not to worry," Johnny announced as the laughter waned. From a vest pocket, he pulled out a fistful of paper money and slapped the wad down on the bar. "When Johnny Hollister says he's got money to spend, he *means* he's got money to spend. So there, you damn stingy Swede! Take what you need and then commence to pushing some thirst quenchers back this direction."

Now the barkeep complied post haste. After nimbly plucking out the payment he required, Jorgeson slid a bottle and a pair of glasses in front of Clancy and Mort and then a second bottle, minus any glass, in front of Johnny. While the two tag-along veterans poured their drinks, knocked them back, and then poured again, Johnny tipped his bottle high and took a long, gurgling swig.

Lowering the bottle with a loud thump and passing the back of his hand across his lips as he emitted a satisfied sigh, Johnny said, "Now that's more like it! Now we're on the right path. The only thing left is seein' to the second powerful craving I came in here to take care of … where are you hiding Bitsy, Jorgeson? Trot her fine little ass out here 'cause my other hankerin' is one that she knows exactly how to satisfy."

A frown pulled Jorgeson's long face a little longer. "Afraid there's a little hitch when it comes to trotting out Bitsy for you," he said. His eyes darted involuntarily toward the doorway-lined hallway at the back of the room before returning to Johnny. "So happens Bitsy is already occupied. Seein's how they went back there only a few minutes ago, the wait is likely going to be a while. You know how Bitsy likes to give a good, long ride for the money."

Johnny's face reddened with an angry scowl. "Aw,

bullshit to that! This hankerin' in me has got too much pressure built up. I'm liable to explode, I tell you."

"Look, I'm sorry," Jorgeson said. "But what can I do? I don't have but two—"

"If they only just went back there," Johnny cut him off, "then they can't be that heavy into things. You go knock on the door and tell the other fella I'll pay for his poke if he let's me go first and get my diddle out of the way. Tell him it's a medical necessity. And that ain't no lie—I might have a stroke or something if I have to hold it in very much longer."

Jorgeson shook his head. "I can't do that. That other fella got here first and already paid his money up front. He's got a right to conduct his business without—"

"Then *I'll* go knock on the damn door and make him a deal," Johnny said, interrupting again.

"No. You won't. I won't allow it," Jorgeson said firmly.

Johnny's face grew redder. "You ain't being very considerate to a paying customer, Jorgeson."

"That's just the point. I *am* being considerate to a paying customer."

"Who is that horny bastard, anyway?"

"Don't know him. He said he's new to these parts."

"So I been comin' here, regular-like, for over a year now yet you give consideration to some damn stranger over *me*?"

"Doggone it, Johnny, that's the way it has to be. It's the fair and proper way to conduct business."

"All right. Speakin' of business," Johnny said through clenched teeth, "maybe it's time I start takin' mine elsewhere. I already know plenty of other fellas who do their drinkin' at that Mex joint over by Peno Junction. It's a little longer ride, but the liquor there is just as good. And cheaper. And maybe their whores don't speak English so hot, but I hear that if you flip 'em face down they squeal just the same and know how to wiggle those fat brown asses to give a hombre a mighty fine poke."

Jorgeson held his ground, expression grim, as he said, "I guess you'll do what you feel you have to, Johnny. And I've got to do the same."

The two men glared at each other for a long, tense minute. Clancy and Mort, the pair of older wranglers, looked on anxiously. Each held a fresh-poured drink in his hand, not knowing if they'd be staying for another round or if they'd be tagging along after Johnny when he stormed out.

Abruptly, Jorgeson relented a bit. "Look," he said. "How about you take a turn with June to, you know, sort of tide you over until Bitsy is available? I'll make it half price for you to let June relieve some of that pressure you've got built up so bad."

Johnny made a pained face and let out a groan. "Aw, come on, man. I didn't show up here for no damn poke with no ugly-ass damn June. Jesus! She was homely as a mud fence to begin with and now, since Hugo Lisle smacked the shit out of her for mouthing off about him doing the same to his ol' lady, she only looks worse. You think I didn't see her when I came in just now? Even that little peek was damn near enough to curdle this load I'm packin'."

"Here now, quiet it down a little bit," Jorgeson protested. He jerked a thumb to indicate the flimsy partition running behind the bar. "June is right there in the back, she can hear every word you're saying."

"So what?" Johnny huffed. "Don't she know what a homely bitch she is? The only reason anybody *ever* paid to diddle her was when they was blind drunk or when the line waiting for Bitsy was too long. And since Big Hoss scarred her up on top of—"

"All right, that does it!" This time it was Jorgeson who did the interrupting and his expression made it pretty clear his patience was used up. "I think you had the right idea before, Johnny, about taking your business elsewhere. Doggone it, I tried to be reasonable with you. But if you won't meet me half way, then I'm tired of trying and I'm tired of your mouth and attitude."

"You're gettin' mighty uppity there, ain't you, Jorgeson?"

"Call it what you want. This is my place and I don't have to take guff off you or anybody else."

"You keep usin' that uppity tone with me, you might find out different."

"Come on, Johnny. It ain't worth it," said Clancy. "Hugo warned us about not comin' into town and causin' a ruckus."

"Yeah, like he's got room to talk," muttered Johnny. Then his eyes flashed and he thrust his chin defiantly toward Jorgeson. "How about that, Mr. Uppity? Bet you didn't try that shit with Hugo 'Big Hoss' Lisle when he was in here the other night bustin' up your ugly goddamn whore and makin' her even uglier. Did you?"

"What happened between me and Hugo is between me and Hugo. The only thing you need to worry about is getting on out of here. Take the bottles you paid for and hit the trail."

"To hell with your stinkin' bottles of booze. I drank the last drop of anything I'm ever going to from this lousy shithole."

"You've got money coming back, then. I won't have it said—"

Johnny waved him off with a jerky wave of one hand. "Keep your lousy money, too! Take the money and the bottles and shove the whole works up your ass for all I care." Then, turning toward the door, he barked over his shoulder to his two companions, "Come on, boys. We're done with this dump."

Mort and Clancy hesitated. They cast sad, longing glances at the bottles slated to be left behind, then threw back the shots they'd already poured and fell in step behind Johnny.

CHAPTER FOUR

Johnny had barely taken a step, however, before he stopped short. So abrupt and unexpected was the move that his two tag-alongs nearly slammed up against him.

As Johnny froze, his eyes locked on The Lawyer, like he'd noticed him for the first time. Specifically, his gaze fell on The Lawyer's hat, where it rested upside down on the bar next to his saddlebags and rifle.

After a moment, without looking around but tossing the words out the side of his mouth and over his shoulder, Johnny said, "'Fore I go, Swede, I all of a sudden got me a question ... Since you've gone and got so uppity about the way you run things around here, how is it you're allowing folks to keep their own personal spittoons right up on the bar top beside 'em. Ain't that pretty damn disgustin'?"

Up to that point, The Lawyer had for the most part been managing—albeit with increasing difficulty—to ignore the loudmouthed Johnny. Now it looked like that option was going to be taken off the table. And damned if he wasn't almost glad.

He swallowed the bite of sandwich he was chewing and turned to face Johnny. "You must mean my hat," he said calmly.

"Your *hat*?" Johnny echoed.

"That's right," confirmed Jorgeson, moving up on the opposite side of the bar. "He had it on when he came in."

"Well that's the goddamnedest excuse for a hat I ever saw!" exclaimed Johnny. "I swear, it looks to me like a spittoon ... or, come to study on it, even more than that like some kind of fancified piss-pot."

"No matter to you. You're leaving. Remember?" Jorgeson reminded him edgily.

"That's okay. The gentleman's entitled to his opinion," The Lawyer said.

"You're partly right, mister. I damn sure am entitled to my opinion," stated Johnny. Then one side of his mouth lifted into a crooked grin. "There's plenty around who'd question *your* opinion when it comes to callin' me a gentleman, though."

Clancy and Mort guffawed obligingly at their comrade's wry humor.

"Nonetheless," The Lawyer said, his voice still calm as he picked up the item in question and held it before him, "this *is* a hat."

Johnny snorted. "Call it what you want. All I got to say is that anybody who'd put a piss pot-lookin' thing like that on their head and go paradin' around in public has got to be either a plumb idiot or some kind of sissy boy."

Jorgeson started to say something but Mort cut him short with a warning look.

"Actually," said The Lawyer, his tone taking on a

somewhat sharper edge, "this not only is a hat, but it's a rather special one. It can be worn as you see it now. Or, for formal occasions such as are admittedly few and far between in this part of the country, with a slight adjustment" —he reached inside the piece of headgear as he was speaking and triggered a hidden button, releasing the crown extension so that it rose another four inches in height— "it can be turned into quite a serviceable top hat."

He ended by swinging the hat up with a flourish and placing it on his head.

Johnny's jaw dropped. For a moment, he didn't seem able to find any words. When he did, he blurted, "I'll be a sonofabitch! That settles it—you *are* a sissy!"

"Funny you should say that." The Lawyer's voice was level, but still with the sharper edge to it. Removing the hat and placing it on the bar once again, he continued. "When you first came parading in, with your strut and your jingly spurs and all those glittering silver conches, I wondered the same about you. Either a mollycoddle or maybe a show pony, I couldn't quite make up my mind. Then, quickly enough, I saw that show pony was the right call—and, by your words and actions, you were even obliging enough to clarify exactly which end."

A tense silence suddenly filled the room and clamped down on everybody there.

All color seemed to momentarily drain from Johnny's face. But then, in sharp contrast, a rush of scarlet anger flooded up over his scowling counte-nance. "Mister," he said, his voice thick and raspy, "if that was supposed to be some kind of lame-assed joke, it might be the biggest and last mistake you ever make. You got about half a second to try and fix that by doing some real serious beggin' your pardon. Elsewise, I'm gonna perforate you with so many holes they'll be able to fold you up, shove you into that piss bucket you call a hat, and haul you out of here in it."

The Lawyer regarded him with a flinty gaze. Then, very slowly and deliberately, he wagged his head. Once to the left, once to the right. "Be a lot smarter idea, Johnny-boy, for you to leave like you were fixing to do. While you can manage under your own power ... you don't, it won't be me who gets hauled out."

But Johnny Hollister wasn't big on smart ideas. He'd demonstrated that fact with unfortunate frequency in the years since he grew out of his teens and came to believe that a fancy gun on his hip made him something more than he was. And he demonstrated it again this night in Jorgeson's saloon when his hand jabbed suddenly downward to try and draw the silver-plated Colt from its black leather holster.

To *try* and draw the Colt ...

The attempt was pitifully short of success. His clawed fingers wrapped around the pearl grips and the six-shooter lifted half an inch out of the leather. But before it cleared any more, the big Remington that had appeared faster than an eye blink in The Lawyer's fist was being thrust toward Johnny, roaring out a tongue of flame and a sizzling bullet that smashed into the younger man's right shoulder and sent him spinning half way around with a yelp of pain.

The Lawyer followed his shot, instantly covering the distance between him and Johnny in a single long stride. As he did this, he swung the Remington in a quick, flat arc that ended with the gun's barrel crashing hard against the side of Johnny's face. The would-be gunman's knees were already starting to buckle from the bullet strike. The added blow caused them to fold the rest of the way and Johnny dropped to the floor in a heap.

While Johnny was still in mid collapse, The Lawyer swung his Remington in another flat arc, this one sweeping its aim over Clancy and Mort. The two tag-along wranglers were poised hump-backed, like they were getting ready to do something, but the movement from The Lawyer froze them like a pair of stone statues.

"No. No more shooting. Please!" urged Jorgeson from his side of the bar.

Abruptly, Clancy and Mort jerked their hands up level with their ears, palms open and empty.

"Christ!" The Lawyer said disgustedly. "Put your stupid hands down and unbuckle your gun belts—slow and easy. Let them drop. Then go over to that far table against the wall and sit down. Keep your hands where I can see them. Stay like that until I tell you otherwise."

The two men did as instructed, all the while under the watchful, threateningly silent eye of The Lawyer's gun muzzle.

Once Mort and Clancy were satisfactorily in place, The Lawyer turned his attention to the three elderly cribbage players seated at the nearer table. All through the outburst of violence, they had stayed totally still and quiet.

"You gents had about enough cribbage-playing for the night?" The Lawyer wanted to know.

Three silently bobbing heads gave him his answer.

"Get out of here, then. Go home and play with your grandkids."

The three oldsters got up and shuffled out the door, leaving their cribbage set on the table but making sure to grab the whiskey bottle and take it with them.

No sooner had the trio disappeared through the front door when a faint click of sound from the opposite end of the room caused The Lawyer to spin around and thrust his gun in that direction, white-knuckled thumb poised on the hammer. Halfway down the doorway-lined hallway at the rear, one of the doors had opened a cautious ten inches and slices of two faces fixed with wary expressions—the much sought after Bitsy and her current customer, The Lawyer guessed—peeked out through the gap.

Easing his thumb off the hammer, The Lawyer spoke in a low, grating voice. "Go on back to your business. You don't want any part of this."

The faces were quickly withdrawn and the door snapped back shut again.

"Jesus, mister," said Jorgeson somewhat breathlessly.

The Lawyer cut him a hard look. "Go get the girl."

"W–what girl?"

"The redhead who brought my sandwiches."

"She doesn't deserve to get dragged into this," Jorgeson protested.

"She already has been. That's the whole point. Now do like I say, dammit."

The bartender retreated to do as ordered, dragging his feet reluctantly.

Careful to keep Mort and Clancy in his peripheral vision and with the Remington at all times gripped in his right fist, The Lawyer knelt down next to the fallen Johnny. With his left hand, he reached and shook the wounded man by his undamaged shoulder. "Wake up, Johnny-boy. Come on, time to rejoin the party you insisted on starting."

Johnny lifted his head slightly and emitted a murmuring groan.

The Lawyer moved his hand and gave a couple light cheek-slaps, just above the raw bruise his slamming gun barrel had made. "Let's go. You're not hurt that bad."

Johnny's eyes fluttered open under furled brows. His mouth twisted into a grimace. "Hey, Goddamn … I'm in pain … I hurt like hell."

"You probably don't hurt as bad as you deserve."

Johnny blinked some more, vision coming into focus on the man looming over him. His brows scrunched into a fierce scowl. "You sonofabitch … you shot me!"

"Just obliging what you seemed in such a hurry for," The Lawyer told him.

Groaning again, louder this time, Johnny lifted himself on his left elbow. He craned his neck and rolled his eyes in order to look down at his oozing, bullet-blasted shoulder. "Good God! I'm hurt bad … I'm hurt real bad. Is the doctor on his way?"

"No need to be in a hurry about bothering the doc. I happen to know he's already got his hands full."

Johnny's eyes whipped back, narrowing, boring into The Lawyer as he fairly screeched, "What do you mean there's no hurry for the doctor? Can't you see I'm bleeding here, you cold-hearted bastard? ... And it ain't just the blood, I can feel my shoulder is all busted to—ah, oh shit, that hurts!"

"Settle down. You're just making it worse, you damn fool."

"You're the one who did this, you bastard. I'm tellin' you, I need a doctor bad!"

"For God's sake, mister," said Mort from the far table, "it ain't human to just leave him layin' there bleedin' and in pain."

The Lawyer pinned him with a hard glare. "Best shut your mouth or you can get a taste of the same."

Jorgeson reappeared behind the bar, the redhead girl next to him. The Lawyer acknowledged them with a quick glance and then cut his eyes back down to Johnny. "You want to get that shoulder tended to before you bleed out? All you have to do is settle down, quit calling names, and take care of a certain chore ... then I'll allow the doctor to be sent for."

Johnny's expression ran the gamut between fear and anger. "Chore? What the hell are you talkin' about? I'm blasted to hell here, mister, I ain't up for doin' no kind of chore."

The Lawyer ignored him and instead swung his attention to the copper-haired girl behind the bar. Once again she stood with her chin tucked down so that her hair spilled forward on the sides, obscuring most of her face. "Miss ... June, is it?" he said in a surprisingly soft, gentle voice. "Come around over here, will you, please."

June lifted her face. For a moment her eyes were wide with uncertainty, a trace of fear. But something in The Lawyer's tone soothed and reassured her. After only another moment's hesitation, she came around the end of the bar and walked over to where The Lawyer remained on one knee beside the wounded Johnny.

The latter watched her move up and come to a halt, standing over him. "What is this? What the hell's going on?" he wanted to know. "What the shit has June got to do with any of this?"

"She had plenty to do with the insulting filth you insisted on spewing only a little while ago," The Lawyer reminded him.

Johnny looked bewildered. "So what? She's nuthin' but a whore—and a goddamn ugly, lousy poke of one, at that. The likes of her deserve to be insulted."

Through clenched teeth, The Lawyer said, "And the likes of her also deserve to be knocked around and battered at the whim of so-called men such as this Big Hoss Lisle you seem so impressed by, too. Is that it?"

"What do you want me to say?" wailed Johnny. "She's a goddamn whore. She deserves whatever she gets."

The Lawyer clamped his free hand over Johnny's wounded shoulder and squeezed hard, until the already shattered bones ground together and crunched loud

39

enough to be heard above the howls of pain. The Lawyer let go after a moment and then waited until Johnny's howls subsided to a few whimpers and gradually only ragged gasps as he tried to catch his breath. June looked on with no emotion—certainly none of remorse or empathy—in her expression.

The Lawyer leaned forward and shoved his face closer to Johnny's, close enough to smell the stink of the clammy sweat that had popped out across the young loudmouth's forehead. In a voice like two coarse stones scraping together, The Lawyer said, "What this girl deserves and is going to get—from *you*, you crude, arrogant little bastard—is some of that real serious begging your pardon you spoke of earlier. An apology for every cruel and hurtful remark you ever made to her. It's going to be the most sincere, heartfelt spill of words to ever came out of that slime hole you call a mouth … you're going to say them to her, but it's *me* you're going to have to convince."

"You go to hell," Johnny hissed.

"That's a foregone conclusion, son. But if you don't do like I say" —The Lawyer held up his hand so Johnny could see the blood smear still there from gripping his bullet-torn shoulder— "I guarantee I'll make you think you're already there."

CHAPTER FIVE

In the morning, after rising early and taking the bath that had gotten postponed the night before, The Lawyer left Jorgeson's building and walked over to Doc Simes's place to call on the Brandywines, as promised. The air was still fresh and crisp at this hour, but the sky was clear and the lifting sun shimmered bright with the promise of the warmth it would bring the new fall day.

As he angled across the unmarked main street of Carstairs Crossing, The Lawyer's thoughts—as they had been ever since waking—were primarily on plans for once again taking up the trail of Lou Crenshaw. But other things skimmed through his mind as well.

The shooting of Johnny Hollister had been of little consequence to him, other than the apology it drew for the tormented saloon girl, June. In retrospect, he recognized the satisfaction from that might have felt nearly as good to him as it had to June herself. He could have just as easily killed Johnny, it would have been a clear case of self-defense. But while he'd ended more than a few lives since starting on the journey of The Lawyer—none with any real remorse—he nevertheless tried to avoid killing whenever possible … the obvious exceptions, of course, would be the remaining vermin who had slaughtered his family. There would be no avoidance there. Them he wanted to kill so bad he ached; an ache he knew would only be relieved once he'd caught up with each and every one.

Also lingering on The Lawyer's mind this morning was how June had come to his room in the small hours after midnight. "You can leave the light off, so you don't have to look at me," she'd said. "But I appreciate you sticking up for me like you did, and to show my gratitude I know some things that I promise you'll really enjoy." He hadn't been with a woman since the loss of his wife. He never allowed himself to feel the need. For some reason it had seemed necessary to take time to explain this to June, revealing to her more of his past than he'd shared with anyone since the slaughter. Then, because by that point he *did* feel the need to be with a woman—though not completely—he motioned her to his bed and, with the lamp turned up high to show her she didn't have to hide the way she looked, they had lain in each other's arms until the dawn.

* * *

"No offense, Doc," The Lawyer said to Simes after he'd been ushered out of the bright morning sunshine and into the medic's office, "but you look a mite used around the edges."

"Comes from a little something called lack of sleep. It hits even harder in advanced years. Hence, since I've been up most of the night—thanks in no small part to you—this is the result."

"Thanks to *me*?" questioned The Lawyer. "The hour was still plenty early last night when I got out of your hair. And I thought Howard Brandywine was well on the mend."

"True on both counts," affirmed the doctor.

"So were there some added complications with him after that, then?"

"Not with Howard, no. He continues to do just fine, in spite of also failing to get the uninterrupted rest I would have preferred." Simes arched a brow. "But are you forgetting that he was only the *first* gunshot victim you sent my way last night?"

The Lawyer frowned. "If you're talking about that young pup Johnny Hollister, I didn't send him no damn where. I could have sent him to the undertaker, though, if I'd wanted. He asked for it by drawing on me and going for his gun first."

"That's what I was given to understand," Simes allowed. "Nevertheless, his pals brought him here to me. Getting the lead out wasn't the problem so much as the bone and joint damage the bullet did."

The Lawyer shrugged. "Sorry for the burden on you, Doc. But don't expect me to care a whole lot about whatever damage he suffered. Like I said, he was on the prod and looking for trouble. I *could* have damaged him permanent."

"I can appreciate that," said Simes, looking thoughtful. "But what I think you need to appreciate is that the trouble Johnny was on the prod for might not have stopped with you putting a bullet in him."

"What's that supposed to mean? Are you saying he

has friends who are going to come after me for what I did to him?"

Simes gave a grunt and twisted his mouth wryly. "I doubt Johnny Hollister has a friend in the world, not discounting those he's spending money on, buying drinks for. You saw enough of him to spot that he's got the personality of a shit-house rat ... but, all the same, he's part of a ranch crew—the Bar Double-T. The ramrod of that outfit is an individual named Hugo Lisle who, believe it or not, has the capacity to be even less charming than young Johnny."

"I keep hearing that name. He's also called 'Big Hoss' Lisle, right?"

"That would be him, yes."

"And part of his charm—or lack thereof, again based on what I've heard—is his habit of beating up women. Like his own wife, on a regular basis, and recently one of Jorgeson's saloon girls, the one called June. Have I got that part right, too?"

"You do," admitted Simes quietly.

"So why the hell doesn't somebody do something about him? If he's only the ramrod of the outfit, doesn't whoever he works for have any say over his actions?"

"The owner of the Double Bar-T is an invalid who seldom leaves the house. I suspect he neither knows nor cares about Hugo's methods as long as the ranch operation runs smoothly and makes a profit."

"So what's the excuse for everybody else? Does Big Hoss have all the men in the territory so buffaloed none of them are willing to stand up to him?"

The doctor looked down, unable to meet his eyes.

"Damn it, none of that has anything to do with the point I'm trying to make."

"What is your point then, Doc? What are you trying to tell me?"

Simes lifted his face. "Look, you showed up on the trail of the villain who shot Howard Brandywine and stole his horses. You did the right thing and gave up your chase for the sake of aiding the Brandywines. That having been done, however, my point is that any further obligation you might feel toward them isn't necessary and you have every right to now pursue your own interests."

"Which is exactly what I intended to do, as soon as I made this promised visit," stated The Lawyer. Then he set his jaw, firmly and visibly. "But I'll be damned if I'll let anyone think that I'm running from the threat of a woman-beater like this Lisle character."

"Hang what anybody thinks!" said Simes irritably. "Besides, only a handful of people even know enough about the circumstances to form an opinion one way or the other. What's more, I'm only speculating that Lisle might feel the need for some kind of retaliation. Comes down to it, he could just as likely take his ire out on young Hollister for acting the way he did. Just to be clear, he's a ruffian who doesn't *only* beat up on women."

"But if Big Hoss *does* feel the nccd to retaliate and I'm not around, then what?" The Lawyer said. "Does he take it out on June because I made her part of it by forcing Johnny to apologize to her? Jorgeson, because it all happened in his place? Maybe even the

45

Brandywines, because getting involved with them and their trouble is what brought me to town in the first place?"

Simes sighed in exasperation. "Like I said—and I'm damned sorry I brought it up at all—whatever Lisle might do or not do is pure speculation on my part. Obviously you know your way around a gun. Maybe it's best if you *do* wait around, then you can just go ahead and kill the bastard if he shows up."

"That'd be a way to make sure he doesn't cause trouble for anybody else."

The doctor's eyes bugged. "Good God, man. I wasn't being serious! Is that really the memory you'd want to leave behind for the people you've gone out of your way to help—the saloon girl and the Brandywines and their new baby? That, in the end, you turned out to be just somebody else on the prod, quick with a gun and quick to use it for killing?"

"If that was the case," The Lawyer argued, "then why didn't I go ahead and kill Johnny Hollister when … wait a minute. Did you just say 'the Brandywines and their new baby'?"

Simes's head bobbed. "That's right. I hadn't got around to mentioning that part yet." He used the back of his hand to try and stifle a yawn. "As a matter of fact, she's the main reason for my lack of sleep. Me and everybody else. She showed up a little before midnight, right after I'd finished with Johnny Hollister, and didn't stop squalling until it was darn near daylight. Judging by the strength of her lungs, she is a very healthy young lady and there is every reason to think she'll stay that way."

The Lawyer smiled as wide a smile as he'd managed since the attack on his family. "I'll be damned ... I mean darn. A little girl, eh? Have they named her yet?"

"I don't think so. Not that I've heard."

"How about the mother? Is she doing okay?"

"Fine." Now the doctor smiled. "Except for a strained eardrum perhaps."

"Is it okay if I go ahead and visit with them for a few minutes? Or, since they only recently got to sleep, maybe it would be best if I didn't interrupt ..."

"No, not at all," Sims assured him. "They've been looking forward to you stopping by. They'd be highly disappointed if you didn't. Follow me, I'll take you back to them."

CHAPTER SIX

The Lawyer spent the better part of an hour with the Brandywines. It proved to be a more relaxed, pleasant visit than any he'd experienced since he couldn't remember when. He even held the infant girl for a little while. Taking the tiny bundle in his arms brought on a sudden rush of familiarity, sadness, and longing. But mostly it felt good, reminding him of the continuum of life and—as opposed to the darker side of humanity where he himself was dwelling these days, stalking those who leaked like a plague out from the even darker depths—the promise and unspoiled sweetness of a new baby.

When the matter of the baby's still undecided name came up again, Eloise surprised him by saying, "We were hoping that maybe you could help us with that. Since it's entirely likely that none of our family would have survived to even be here today if you hadn't come along when you did, we'd be honored if you would suggest a name, perhaps that of a special lady from your life or one significant to you for whatever reason."

For a moment, The Lawyer was caught at a loss for words. But then, looking down at the little charmer with a headful of thick, dark hair and her mother's almond skin, the answer came to him with abrupt ease.

"You could do worse," he said somewhat huskily, "than to call her Ahnaleesha … it comes from my late wife. She was a full-blooded Cheyenne, so it's an Indian name. Roughly translated, it means Beautiful Hair of Midnight."

"Ahnaleesha … Ahnaleesha Brandywine," Eloise repeated softly, looking from her daughter to her husband. "I like it."

Howard nodded. "Ahnaleesha … yeah, it's got a right pretty ring to it."

"Of course," The Lawyer said, "since it's an Indian name, I'd understand if you'd rather not—"

"Don't be ridiculous," Eloise said sternly. "It's a perfectly lovely name and it's settled. Ahnaleesha Brandywine it is!"

* * *

The Lawyer left the Brandywines and Doc Simes in an unusually good mood. He knew the feeling wouldn't last, though, and that was fitting. He'd resigned himself long ago to neither deserving nor wanting to feel good in any lasting, general sense. Not until the grim task of tracking down his family's butchers was finished. After that, if he survived, what outlook he'd take for the remainder of his life would have to be determined.

As he re-crossed the town's main street, headed back toward Jorgeson's saloon, The Lawyer began once more focusing his thoughts on starting anew after Lou Crenshaw. He was confident he'd manage to catch up with the murderous dog again, regardless of the lead Crenshaw was certain to have established by now. The Lawyer's relentless tenacity would always give him an edge, no matter what else. What was more, he'd already spoken with Huffman, the livery proprietor, when he stalled Redemption last night, and arranged for him to have one of his sturdiest horses ready this morning for The Lawyer to purchase as a spare mount of his own.

As he walked, The Lawyer took notice that the business district of Carstairs Crossing, the brunt of which stretched for two or three blocks on down from this northern end, was bustling with considerably more activity than it had been earlier. The community had the feel of a place that was destined to thrive and one day become a decent place for decent folks to live in and around. A good trading center for the Brandywines to be near as they made a go of their fledgling farm, and a good place for little Ahnaleesha to grow, go to school, and one day start breaking the hearts of all the young bucks in the territory.

Because Jorgeson's wasn't yet open for business, The Lawyer started down the narrow alley that ran along the south side of the building, separating it from the grain warehouse next door, aiming for the rear entrance he'd used when he left to go see the Brandywines. He'd only gone a few steps, however, when he suddenly had company in the narrow passageway. Directly ahead, at the far end of the saloon building, a man appeared. The Lawyer immediately recognized him as Clancy, one of the wranglers who'd been in the company of Johnny Hollister last night.

Leaning out around the corner, Clancy extended his right arm forward in a kind of stabbing motion toward The Lawyer. In the fist at the end of the arm was gripped a short-barreled Colt revolver. Without saying a word, Clancy pulled the trigger.

Lost in thought though he'd been, The Lawyer had nevertheless gotten alerted to the possibility of something being wrong a scant fraction of a second before Clancy fully appeared. The slight movement of the wrangler's hat brim sliding out and then back in behind the corner of the building, as he'd made a preliminary peek before committing himself, had registered on some level and sent a warning tingle that was still running through The Lawyer even as the gun was brought to bear on him. It was enough to kick his reflexes into gear and send him pitching down and to his left as the blast of Clancy's shot filled the alley.

The bullet streaked close along the side of the building, hitting nothing, and plowed into the dirt out in the middle of the street. In the same instant, The Lawyer hit the ground on his left shoulder, rolled quickly toward the warehouse side of the alley, and came up on one knee with his own gun drawn and raised. He snapped off two rapid-fire shots before Clancy could redirect his aim. The first slug from The Lawyer's Remington angled up under Clancy's armpit and blew through the pad of meat and muscle at the back, causing Clancy to fling his arm out wide and the revolver to go flying from his grasp. The second bullet crashed through the would-be ambusher's rib cage, this time busting bone and cartilage. Clancy spun half way around and pitched face down, flailing and screeching in pain.

The Lawyer glided to his feet, eyes sweeping alertly, gun muzzle moving in unison. Where there was an apparently vengeance-seeking Clancy, The Lawyer warned himself, then it seemed reasonable to anticipate that Mort probably wasn't far behind.

The answer came soon enough.

From directly across the street, out of a tangle of underbrush and stunted trees nearly engulfing a weathered, half-collapsed old shed, a rifle barked and a bullet sizzled into the alley, whacking against the side of the warehouse. The Lawyer heard the unmistakable *thurrp!* and even felt the lick of heat on his skin as the slug passed less than an inch from his cheek. He wheeled about, dropping into a low crouch, and returned fire blindly, instinctively, throwing another pair of shots in the general direction of the shed.

But this bought only a moment's reprieve before the rifleman (almost certain to be Mort, even though he remained unseen) responded by pouring more bullets into the alley. With slugs whining dangerously close and no cover available in the gap between buildings, The Lawyer's only recourse was to turn and break into a zigzagging run, attempting to try and make it around a corner of one of the structures. Bullets chased his every step.

From where he still lay on the ground, writhing in agony, Clancy's wordless wailing turned into desperate shouts and curses. "Goddamn you, Mort, watch where you're shooting! Hold your fire, for Chrissakes, some of those bullets are damn near hitting me!"

The Lawyer couldn't tell for sure whether or not Clancy's protests slowed the rifle fire, but one way or the other he managed to make it around the corner of the saloon building—leaping over Clancy's prone form in the process—without getting hit. He collapsed against the rear outer wall of Jorgeson's, fighting to catch his breath as his hands instantly, automatically went to work reloading the Remington. He also reached out and snagged Clancy's fallen Colt from where it had landed when it sailed out of the wrangler's out-flung grasp.

"Did I get that sonofabitch, Clancy?" Mort called from across the street.

"You damn near finished the job on me, I'll tell you that much!"

"Yeah, yeah, I heard your bitching the first time. But what about that dandy in the piss-pot hat?"

Clancy twisted around painfully and craned his neck to look over at The Lawyer. "No," he called back to Mort. "I don't know how the hell you missed him with all the lead you were pouring in, but I don't see a scratch on him!"

"How did *I* miss him?" Mort said plaintively. "I'm clear the hell across the street—how did *you* miss him when he was practically in your lap?"

"Knock it off, you two magpies," The Lawyer interjected. "The point is, I'm still alive and kicking and I've already cut your desperate duo in half. I've cut you down by two thirds, in fact, if you take into account what I did to Johnny last night ... do I have to put a bullet in you, too, Mort? Or are you going to be the smart one and call a quit to this before you take your own turn at the risk of lead poisoning?"

"Don't let him bluff you, Mort," said Clancy through pain-gritted teeth. "You know what Big Hoss threatened to do to us if we don't settle the score for Johnny … besides, you got the bulge on this hombre. You got the rifle and the best cover. Let him make a try for you and show him what's what."

"Yeah, you do that, Mort. Don't let me bluff you," The Lawyer echoed mockingly. "You go right ahead and form a good plan on how you're going to show me what's what. I wouldn't advise taking too long, though. Not if you want your buddy to still be around to see how you pull it off. Me, I'm in no particular hurry. But whether Clancy knows it or not, he's pumping blood like a stuck hog. Every second we take pondering on how we're going to finish this thing is more blood he's irrigating the ground with."

"Is he right, Clancy?" Mort wanted to know. "Are you hit that bad?"

"He got me twice," Clancy admitted, his voice sounding more subdued and edged with concern. "One of 'em ain't much, but the other, yeah, I'm losin' a lot of blood."

"Can't you clamp a hand or something over it to stop the bleeding?"

"I–I don't think so. Bullet tore through my ribs … feels like I'm leakin' in a couple different places. Can't cover the spread. You'd better make a move pretty quick, pard."

"God damn it all!" Mort's voice grew strident with anguish and frustration. "You in the piss-pot hat—why don't you step out where I can see you? You're comin' on like some kind of big time gun slick, why don't you fight like a man? Step out in the open. I'll do the same. Let's go ahead and finish this."

But The Lawyer didn't answer. At least not right away.

He made no reply because he was on the move. While Mort and Clancy had been yammering back and forth, he'd slipped away so as not to draw Clancy's attention. Gripping the reloaded Remington in his right fist and the confiscated Colt in his left, he crossed the back side of the saloon building and then cut around the opposite corner from where he'd been. He broke into a run again, no zigzag pattern this time, just a straight dash up the alley on this side that passed between Jorgeson's and a small wood frame building that housed a print shop, the only other business on this end of town except for the livery stable catty-cornered across the street. Like the saloon, the printer wasn't yet open for business.

At the street end of the alley, The Lawyer ducked in behind a rain barrel that had been positioned there. It was a huge old wooden hogshead, thick-walled and chest high when stood on end like it was, capable of holding over a hundred gallons of liquid. At this particular point in time, the end of a dry summer, it was empty.

As The Lawyer settled in back of the hogshead, Mort was calling again from across the street. "Answer me, damn you! What do you say? You man enough to face me, straight-up, and finish this?"

From his new vantage point, The Lawyer had a good angle on the dilapidated old shed all but smothered in underbrush and trees. There were two vacant windows peering out through the faded fall foliage. The Lawyer couldn't determine if Mort's voice was coming from one of them or from somewhere in the thick brush. Now that he had a chance to survey the situation without exposing himself, he'd been hoping for a sign, an indicator that would give him a target. But he was anxious to get this over with, too, so rather than simply wait for Mort to reveal himself, he decided to go ahead and try to draw him into it.

"That's rich," he finally responded, "talking about making this a straight-up fight after you two yellow curs tried to ambush me in a crossfire!"

The ploy worked. Surprised by The Lawyer's voice coming from a new location, Mort's reaction resulted in the barrel of his Winchester flashing in one of the empty windows as he shifted his position inside the shed.

The Lawyer didn't hesitate to take advantage of the revelation. He triggered his Remington, sending three rounds slamming through the gaping maw of the window where he'd seen the rifle barrel.

There was a moment of cursing and thrashing about inside the rickety structure. Then Mort's voice hollered angrily, "For the love of Christ, Clancy, why the hell didn't you tell me he was on the move?"

But there was no reply from Clancy.

After several ticks of silence, The Lawyer speculated Clancy must have passed out from his wounds. It had been no exaggeration to say he was hurt bad and losing a serious amount of blood. On the other hand, The Lawyer found himself second guessing his assumption that Clancy was injured beyond being able to mount any kind of further attack. It might have been smarter to make sure of that, he thought now, rather than leave a potential threat behind him. Pausing in the act of once more thumbing fresh rounds into the Remington, The Lawyer twisted around and threw a quick glance back down the length of the alley. But there was nothing there, no sign of a limping, leaking Clancy trying to sneak up on him, and he felt a little foolish for allowing himself the distraction.

Returning his focus to the old shed and the man he now knew was inside, The Lawyer called, "Looks like you're strictly on your own now, Mort. I fear your pal Clancy has checked out. You claimed you wanted it straight-up, just you and me? Well, that's what you've got, you lying, back-shooting scum. How do you like it?"

Mort responded quickly and loudly, trying to cover the slight quaver in his voice with volume. "I like it just fine, you fancified bastard! I ain't afraid of you, not one damn bit!"

So saying, the tip of his rifle barrel poked out the second window—instead of the one where it had briefly appeared before—and four rapid-fire rounds came screaming across the street and into The Lawyer's alley. One slug whined high, one tore into the dirt, two smacked square into the rain barrel. Leaning against the oversized cask on the opposite side, The Lawyer felt the sturdy, curved wooden slats shiver in concert with hollow-sounding thumps from the impacts. But nothing came close to penetrating through.

This gave The Lawyer an idea. A wild notion, to be sure, but one he quickly and firmly made up his mind to act on.

After giving the hogshead a nudge with his shoulder and feeling it wobble obligingly, The Lawyer re-holstered the Remington and temporarily jammed Clancy's Colt into his waistband. Then, getting a wide grip with his freed hands along the barrel's rim, he began rocking it back and forth until he had it tilting enough to tip it completely onto one side. Even thus overturned, the massive cask still rose to a height well above his waist, continuing to provide good cover.

Staying in a crouch, half expecting Mort to lay down another volley at any second, The Lawyer hitched the hogshead around a bit until he had it positioned just how he wanted it. Then he leaned into it and set it to rolling, all the while ducked in close behind.

The great barrel rolled out of the alley and onto the edge of the street, rumbling dully as it picked up momentum, headed on a course straight for the brush-choked old shed. Yellow dust boiled up and filled The Lawyer's nostrils as he stayed low behind his mobile cover, repeatedly giving it shoves and then breaking into an awkward, bent-over trot in order to keep up.

Now the expected volley came from Mort, the hail

of slugs hammering the hogshead without doing any serious damage as it shivered and trembled and bounced over the wagon ruts in the middle of the street. When there was a pause in the Winchester fire, The Lawyer was ready. Drawing both of the handguns, he straightened up behind the still-rolling barrel, extended his arms out ahead of him with the Remington once again in his right fist and the Colt in his left, and began firing each in an alternating rhythm. His slugs slapped and whacked loudly against the weathered gray husk of the rickety building, forcing Mort to stay hunkered somewhere out of sight.

At the last minute, as the barrel rolled the rest of the way and banged to a halt under the empty black holes of the windows, The Lawyer veered off and lunged toward the opposite end of the truncated structure. There was a sagging, crookedly hanging door there—little more than a handful of unevenly-spaced vertical planks—that he threw his full weight against. The planks fell away with minimal resistance and went rattling off into the murky, shadow-cut interior. The Lawyer burst in after them, guns still raised and ready. When Mort loomed out of the shadows to his right, swinging up the Winchester, attempting to re-center its aim, The Lawyer fired both revolvers simultaneously and blew his legs out from under him.

CHAPTER SEVEN

Clancy didn't make it.

By the time the shooting was over and townsfolk had begun trickling out onto the street again and Doc Simes was summoned, the hapless wrangler lay dead from blood loss in the alley where he'd fallen. His accomplice, Mort, fared better though in all likelihood would be walking on crutches or at least with the aid of a cane for the rest of his days.

The local undertaker's wagon came and took away Clancy's body. As instructed by the doctor, a couple of men carried Mort out of the old shed and laid him on the ground at the edge of the street where Simes opened his medical bag and gave initial attention to the wounded legs.

While all of this was playing out, The Lawyer went over and sat down on the edge of the boardwalk in front of Jorgeson's saloon. June brought him out a bottle of whiskey from which he took occasional sips as he kept a wary eye on the proceedings around him. Quite a crowd had gathered by that point, those comprising it showing their own measure of wariness by keeping a good distance back from where he sat.

After a while, Huffman, the livery proprietor, walked up and said, "I looked out as soon as the shooting started and heard and saw enough to figure out those two jaspers were trying to catch you in a crossfire ambush. Everything you did was in self-defense. I'll tell that to anybody who wants to know."

The Lawyer nodded. "Appreciate that."

Huffman's brow furled. "I–I reckon I should have done something to try and help you ... but it all happened so fast I couldn't decide what it should be."

"No need to explain. Don't worry about it," The Lawyer told him.

Huffman's eyes widened. "But the way you rolled that big ol' barrel across the street and went in behind it a-blazin' with two guns ... dang! That was something to see."

The Lawyer took a drink of whiskey and made no reply.

Across the way, a buckboard pulled up and some men carefully loaded Mort onto it. Doc Simes motioned them in the general direction of his office, where he presumably would follow and provide additional and more thorough treatment. Before that, however, he picked up his bag and came over to The Lawyer.

"You sure you didn't catch any stray chunks of flying lead or other injuries in that fracas?" he wanted to know.

"All I got," The Lawyer answered, "was the ruination of the bath I took earlier this morning when I had to go rolling around in that alley for the sake of *avoiding* any stray bits of flying lead."

Simes wagged his head. "Boy, you are a wonder."

"Ain't he just," agreed June, who had remained to take a seat on the boardwalk beside The Lawyer after bringing him out the bottle of whiskey. Jorgeson had also come out from inside and stood leaning against one of the support posts for the shingled overhang that ran across the front of his saloon.

The Lawyer now extended the bottle toward the doctor. "Here. You look like you could use this as much or more than me."

Simes took the offering somewhat hesitantly. Arching a brow, he said, "It's scarcely past breakfast, you know."

One corner of The Lawyer's mouth lifted in a weary ghost of a smile. "So what's your point?"

"None. None at all." The doctor lifted the bottle and took a generous swig.

As he was doing this, The Lawyer's gaze made another sweep of the faces in the crowd that continued to hover close but not too close. When Simes lowered the bottle and handed it back, The Lawyer said, "I'm glad you didn't allow the Brandywines to venture out and see this."

Simes said, "Howard is still in no condition to get out of bed and venture anywhere. And Eloise needed to stay with him and the baby. But you're right, they're better off not being here." He shot his own glance toward the milling townspeople. "Too bad there are so many nosy parkers who *do* feel the need to come gawking."

"They have a right. It's their town," The Lawyer

said. "I'm just the stranger who showed up and started shooting hell out of everything."

"I warned you about a possible retaliation for what happened with Johnny Hollister last night," said Simes. "But I didn't expect it to be this way. I figured it would more likely come from Hugo Lisle."

The Lawyer's eyes narrowed. "He may not have had a direct hand in this but, judging by the exchange between Mort and Clancy that I overheard, he was still the one behind it. He's the one who sent them to settle the score for Johnny."

"That's right. I also overheard as much," confirmed Jorgeson. "I wasn't in a position to poke my nose out and see exactly what was going on, for fear of getting my head blown off. But I can back up Smith on those two ambushers saying how it was Hugo who sent them."

Simes fixed his gaze on The Lawyer. "I've got to get over to my office and finish taking care of Mort, no matter if he's an ambusher or not. I only did the minimum necessary here before having him moved to more suitable conditions. There's still a bullet needing to be dug out and a fractured bone or two to set."

"Understood, Doc. Go do what you have to."

"What about you?" Simes said. "There's nothing keeping you from leaving, too. Every indicator is that you only acted in self-defense, so you're clear to go. Should any question arise later, you'll be leaving two men, two well-known local citizens, willing to back up your side of things."

"You seem to be trying awful hard to get rid of me."

"I just don't want there to be any more trouble. Not for you, not for anybody. Plus you've still got your personal business to take care of—the business that got interrupted when you stopped to help the Brandywines to begin with."

The Lawyer's expression went tight. "Nobody needs to remind me about my personal business, Doc. But apparently what you need reminding of is the fact that if Big Hoss Lisle decides to be stubborn about dishing out payback for what happened to his boys—two more now, instead of just the one from last night—then me being out of the picture might not be enough to stop him from retaliating some other way. We've already talked about this. From everything I've heard about the man, he's not exactly fussy who or what he—"

Simes interrupted, saying, "If he does, this town was dealing with Hugo Lisle long before you showed up."

"And doing a damned poor job of it, if you ask me," said The Lawyer.

"Plus, Hugo's bullying ways never involved guns before," pointed out Jorgeson.

"Just because these two cowards this morning decided to try and settle their score with guns," argued Simes, "doesn't mean that's what Hugo sent them to do."

"All the same," said The Lawyer, "he *did* send them."

"That still doesn't mean you're obligated to stick around and fight any more battles for us," Simes insisted. "*If* it even comes to that. Hugo isn't a complete Neanderthal. With you gone and three of his men already out of commission, the odds are at least even he'll see the sense in cutting his losses and not pushing things any farther."

"You may be right, you may be wrong," spoke up Huffman. "But I think we're all about to find out the answer pretty quick. Look off yonder to the north ... if I ain't mistaken, that appears to be Big Hoss and a couple more Bar Double-T wranglers ridin' in now."

CHAPTER EIGHT

It was easy to see why Hugo Lisle was called "Big Hoss." Simply put, he was damn near the size of one—and the plow-pulling variety at that. This assessment by The Lawyer was promptly followed by a pang of sympathy for the straining Appaloosa the big man was astride as he and the two other riders came trotting into town and reined up in front of Jorgeson's saloon.

Lisle rocked back in his saddle, thumbed the brim of his slouch hat higher up on his forehead, and scowled at everything and everybody in general. He was massive across the shoulders, heavy-gutted and heavy-jowled, with an unruly growth of sideburns that obscured his ears and made his face and head appear unnaturally broad, almost as wide as his shoulders. Above his many-times-broken nose, his eyebrows grew as profusely as his sideburns, connecting in the middle to form a single shaggy ledge over piggy little eyes that glinted darkly with menace and distrust.

"What the hell's goin' on here?" he growled to no one in particular. "Looks like somebody's whippin' up a revival meetin' or a lynching or some such—only I don't see no Bibles and I don't see no hang rope."

Doc Simes, who apparently served as a spokesman of sorts for the whole town, answered him. "We've had a spot of trouble here this morning, Hugo. And I'm afraid it involved a couple of Bar Double-T riders."

Lisle's scowl intensified. "Seems to me this town is startin' to make a habit of causin' trouble for my riders. That's what I rode in to check on. I sent a couple men ahead, before first light, to settle a leftover problem from last night. I ain't seein' them anywhere, either … you tellin' me they're the ones involved in this new trouble?"

"If you mean Mort and Clancy, then the answer is yes."

"So where are they?"

The crowd gathered in the street seemed to shrink back in anticipation of what the answer was going to be.

Simes cleared his throat. "Mort has just been taken to my office, where I need to go and attend further to him … Clancy, I regret to say, is at the undertaker's."

"What the hell happened to 'em?" Lisle demanded. As the question exploded loudly out of him his eyes cut meaningfully toward The Lawyer.

Simes started to respond but The Lawyer stopped him with a chopping motion of one hand. Rising to his feet, his own eyes meeting Lisle's glare, he said, "*I* happened to them. Judging by the way you're looking at me, you already had a pretty good idea of that."

"That stupid-looking pile of garbage on top of your head marks you pretty clearly," Lisle said through clenched teeth.

"Uh-huh. Just as your warm and friendly disposition marks you."

"Me and this disposition have been getting by in these parts just fine for a good long spell, buster."

"I don't think you'd have to look very hard to find some disagreement on the 'just fine' part," The Lawyer said. "However long you've been carrying around that chip on your shoulder has been too long."

"Says you. I don't hear nobody else speakin' up." As if challenging any rebuttal to this, Lisle's glare raked across the faces of the others who stood around The Lawyer in front of Jorgeson's and then swung to cover those in the crowd. Yet again, the latter seemed to shrink back somewhat.

"All right," said The Lawyer. "Then the voice of dissent is mine alone. As well as the rest of it. I'm the one who shot Johnny Hollister last night—after he tried to draw on me first. And a little while ago, after they first attempted to trap me in a crossfire ambush, I shot Mort and Clancy. So, if you've got a grievance over how your men have been treated, it's strictly with me. Not this town or anybody else in it."

"You damn right I got a beef with you," Lisle snarled.

The Lawyer nodded. "Fine. Let's get to it then."

Lisle's snarl turned into a sneer. "You're anxious to shoot me, too, is that it? Guess you fancy yourself some kind of gun slick, so that's your answer to everything. But in case you ain't noticed, I'm not packing a sidearm." He spread the front of his sheepskin-lined

69

coat to demonstrate the fact.

"Yet you have no problem with your riders going armed and even sent Mort and Clancy to 'settle the score' with me by setting up an ambush."

"You damn right I sent them to settle the score with you. The way the yellow dogs should have done to begin with last night, after you goaded Johnny and then cut him down! But I never told 'em to ambush you."

"I see. You just never told them not to."

"What's done is done. Water under the bridge. The here and now of this has fallen to me and you," Lisle said forcefully. "I may keep a rifle in my saddle boot for rattlers and other varmints out in the brush, but otherwise my way of settlin' a beef is to do it like a man—with these babies." In another demonstration, he held up two balled fists the size of early pumpkins.

His tone filled with disdain, The Lawyer said, "Yeah, I've heard how especially good you are at using those 'babies' on frail women."

"To hell with that!" Bright red color crawled up Lisle's thick neck and flooded his face. "You do some checkin' around, you'll find plenty of men all through this area who've suffered busted skulls from goin' up against me. The only question now is whether or not you've got the balls to find out first hand."

Several ticks of dead silence settled over the scene and gripped the crowd who looked on motionless.

And then The Lawyer replied. "Fine," he said, starting to unbuckle his gun belt. "All you have to do to find out is haul your fat ass down out of that saddle."

Now a visible ripple of excitement passed through

the crowd. Some of those within it even edged forward a bit. The people gathered around The Lawyer in front of the saloon, however, looked equally as doubtful as excited.

"You sure you know what you're doing?" muttered Huffman as he reached to take The Lawyer's hat and stripped-away gun belt.

"I'm going to expose this bullying tub of guts for the fraud he really is," The Lawyer assured him.

He didn't bother elaborating that he was a practiced orator, taught to argue even the flimsiest of cases confidently and convincingly in front of a jury. In this instance, he could only hope that his cause had more than flimsy substance. How successful he'd be would hinge on the question of whether or not Lisle had any fighting technique beyond the obvious raw strength one would naturally expect from somebody his size. If he did, The Lawyer might be in trouble. On the other hand, if the big man was just a smasher and a brawler, then The Lawyer figured he'd be on at least equal footing by virtue of the training he'd gotten from a law school classmate who'd done a good deal of prizefighting before deciding to wage his battles in the legal arena rather than a boxing ring.

However, once Lisle had climbed down off the Appaloosa, shrugged out of his heavy coat, and came lumbering forward with his fists raised menacingly, The Lawyer couldn't help but feel a tremor of doubt over what the hell he'd let himself in for. Nevertheless, he raised his own fists and began circling, rolling his shoulders to get loose, flexing his legs, bouncing up on the balls of his feet.

"You gonna go into some kind of dance, or are you gonna fight?" Lisle growled.

"For starters," The Lawyer said, "I thought I'd do something like *this*!" On the final word, he suddenly closed the gap between them, snapped two lightning-quick jabs to the side of Lisle's face, then bounded back out of reach as the big man threw a whistling round-house that hit nothing but air. The missed punch pulled Lisle off balance and caused him to stumble awkwardly for a moment before he got reset and turned again to face The Lawyer as the latter went back to circling.

The Lawyer smiled thinly. Too early to say for certain, he cautioned himself, but every indication was that Lisle had no technique. A smasher and brawler, just like he'd figured. Hoped. And if he couldn't close the gap and get his hands on The Lawyer, then a series of slicing, punishing blows combined with that sagging gut rapidly sucking the air out of him would accomplish doing what for too long Lisle had been convincing too many people couldn't be done.

Patient, that's what The Lawyer forced himself to be. The urge was there to smash and pound Lisle's face, to turn it into an even grislier version of June's bruised features and what The Lawyer could only imagine the man's own wife had looked like on more than one occasion. Not to mention the men Big Hoss had beaten to gain his reputation. There was no doubt he was the type who, when he had a man down, would slam and batter until there was nothing left but a bloody pulp.

But The Lawyer stayed with the smarter plan of

jabbing and dodging and letting Lisle help to wear himself down. Every time the big man missed with a powerful swing or reached to grab with his bearlike paws only to come up empty, it took its toll right along with the slicing jabs and the body shots The Lawyer began landing through the openings presented by Big Hoss's frustrated, increasingly off-balance lunges. The few times any of Lisle's blows did hit, they were—thankfully—only glancing strikes. Even at that, the power behind them was enough to jar The Lawyer down to his heels and make him realize if he ever allowed himself to get caught fully by one it would have a devastating effect.

The crowd of onlookers grew stunned to near silence.

As they watched, both of Lisle's eyes puffed shut to where he could barely see out of them. Strings of bloody snot hung from his nostrils and his mouth was a smear of scarlet. His knees sagged, threatening to buckle completely each time The Lawyer's fists flicked a set of jabs or slammed a shuddering body blow. Still, Lisle managed to stay upright. But every time he swung one of his thick arms in an attempt to hit back it seemed to be more ineffective, moving in slower and slower motion.

Much as Lisle was feared and despised by practically everyone in or around Carlisle Crossing, a curious trace of sadness, maybe even pride, seemed to play across a few expressions on the otherwise shocked faces of those watching.

Finally, The Lawyer closed in to finish it. A

shattering right hook, an uppercut, and then another right hook at last sent Lisle crashing to the ground. He lay still, making no attempt to try and get up.

The Lawyer stood over the fallen man for long minute. Feet planted wide, chest heaving, bloodied fists hanging at his sides.

The two Bar Double-T wranglers who'd ridden in with Lisle remained on their horses. They shifted restlessly in their saddles and exchanged looks, as if mutely questioning each other whether they should do something.

Standing nearby, Huffman, the liveryman, calmly drew the Remington from the gun belt he was holding for The Lawyer and said in a low voice, "Just sit easy, boys ... just sit easy."

The two men looked relieved and perfectly willing to follow his advice.

In the middle of the street, having caught his breath, The Lawyer raised his face and swung his gaze in a wide, slow arc to cover all those looking so quietly on.

Then he spoke.

"Well. There he is ... Big Hoss. The woman beater. The intimidator who made you look away in fear and made God knows how many of you even crawl. Nothing but a classic, pathetic bully. Yet you let him get away with it. You all ought to be ashamed. You've got the makings of a good town here. A decent community. But it takes work, it takes pulling together, and it means not ever just standing by and letting anything or anybody poison the good out of it. You let that happen again, you'll deserve whatever you get."

* * *

The sun had scarcely begun its afternoon descent when The Lawyer rode out of Carstairs Crossing. He headed due north, toward the Brandywine farm, to where he would again pick up the trail of Lou Crenshaw.

Redemption was rested and anxious to get out in open country. Additionally, as promised, Huffman had a sturdy, spirited mustang ready to serve as a switch-off mount. When it came to payment, he refused, saying, "The lesson you taught this town, the show you put on … that's payment a-plenty. Take the mustang. Ride it hard. And finish whatever it is you need to do."

Other than that, there wasn't much else said. No anguished goodbyes, no pleas to stay on, no thank-yous or speeches beyond what The Lawyer had already given.

Hugo Lisle eventually got helped to his feet by his men and promptly rode off without comment, licking his wounds but refusing any aid from the doctor. One of the wranglers with him said they'd send a wagon back for Mort after Simes was done patching him up.

Putting the town behind him, The Lawyer wondered briefly if he'd made any difference, if anything would change. But he didn't dwell on the thought for long. Other than wishing the best for the Brandywines and little Ahnaleesha (if they even stuck with the name) he realized he didn't actually care all that much.

He couldn't afford to.

He had to keep everything in him concentrated on the one matter of any real importance: Tracking down and killing the butchers who'd wiped out his family.

Crenshaw would be the next step in accomplishing that. As he considered this, refocusing on the name and the man running not so far out ahead of him, The Lawyer realized something else. While he might never know the answer to the question of whether or not he'd done the town of Carstairs Crossing any lasting good, it was bitter irony that the one person who for certain had benefited from the time he'd spent there was none other than Crenshaw ... for him, The Lawyer's distraction by the Brandywines and subsequent events had amounted to a stay of execution.

But only a temporary one, The Lawyer promised himself grimly.

Only temporary ...

†

ABOUT THE AUTHOR

 Wayne Dundee lives in the once-notorious old cowtown of Ogallala, on the hinge of Nebraska's panhandle. A widower, retired from a managerial position in the magnetics industry, Dundee now devotes full time to his writing.

To date, Dundee has had nearly a score of novels and novellas plus over thirty short stories published. Much of his work has featured his PI protagonist, Joe Hannibal (celebrating over thirty years on the fictional detective scene and appearing most recently in Blade of the Tiger, 2013). He also dabbles in fantasy and straight crime, and lately has done some notable work in the Western genre. His 2010 Western short story, "This Old Star," won a Peacemaker Award from the Western Fictioneers writers' organization. His 2011 novel Dismal River won a Peacemaker in the Best First Western Novel category. His 2012 story "Adeline" won a third Peacemaker, again in the short story category.

Titles in the Hannibal series have been translated into several languages and nominated for an Edgar, an Anthony, and six Shamus Awards. Dundee is also the founder and original editor of *Hardboiled Magazine*.

If you enjoyed reading The Lawyer's adventures, you might also like these Cash Laramie novellas by Wayne D. Dundee. Available from BEAT to a PULP books at www.beattoapulp.com.

಼ಌಜ

Cash Laramie makes his way down the side of a mountain with a prisoner in tow and two prostitutes eager to flee a mining town that's gone bust, looking to make a new life for themselves. An early winter storm promises to make the journey more than a normal struggle. And, leaving town with two of its most precious gems, the prostitutes, puts Cash in the crosshairs of an angry gang of men who are willing to keep the women in town ... at any cost.

U.S. Marshal Cash Laramie is sent out to locate a shipment of stolen guns in the Vedauwoo area of Wyoming where the rocky terrain is treacherous and enshrouded in mystical beauty. In his quest, Cash goes up against an amoral opportunist looking to stir up discord in the region by selling the weapons to a group of Native Americans.

It's been weeks since the famed "Outlaw Marshal" has been heard from. Meanwhile, at the Federal Marshal headquarters in Cheyenne, Wyoming, some disturbing reports are starting to filter in about the notorious Driscoll Gang rapidly hitting a series of banks, allegedly with the aid of a badge-wearing accomplice claiming to be Laramie. Can it be true? Can it be that the lawman with the hair-trigger temper and the mile-wide independent streak has finally gone completely rogue?

The Lawyer made his first appearance in the following Cash Laramie short story originally published in the collection *Protectors: Stories to Benefit PROTECT* and also in *Adventures of Cash Laramie and Gideon Miles*.

THE LAWYER
by Edward A. Grainger

A trail of blood flowed downstream, pulled by the lazy current of the Louisiana bayou. Slowly it dissolved into the muddy water, telling every creature with olfactory organs that a human was helpless and bleeding some-where upstream; they could taste the fear. A raccoon dipped its meal of shellfish into the bayou, then sniffed at the smell of raw human blood. It licked at the clam. Washed it again. Sniffed. Dropped the morsel and retreated into the woods. A water moccasin cut across the dissipating blood, wigging its way toward the far bank. A snout pushed upstream, breathing in the bloody scent, followed by a sinuous body and long serpentine tail. Not much blood can be shed in a Louisiana bayou without a gator coming to investigate.

A thick-muscled body lay on the bayou embankment, bound hand and foot, the source of the blood that drew the alligator. The reptile slowed, wary of the upright human standing over the blood source.

The man they called The Lawyer knelt by the bleeding giant. While his stature didn't measure up to that of the unconscious blacksmith, the Lawyer had the fire of revenge on his side. He worked his fingers into the matted mass of the blacksmith's brown, shoulder-length hair. He jerked the unconscious man's head back, exposing the throat with its prominent larynx. The gator fastened its eyes on the prize and wiggled a little closer.

The Lawyer rolled the big man over. His head lolled, blood still making a pathway down his face from a horribly broken nose. The Lawyer slapped him. It wouldn't do for the blacksmith to die. That would be too easy for him. Another slap. And another.

The eyes fluttered. The Lawyer leaned down to shout in the blacksmith's ear. "Wake. Up. You turtle shit. Wake. Up!"

The blacksmith gurgled. He opened one eye, just a sliver. He saw the Lawyer. He cringed. "No. No. Not again. No. Don't. Mister, don't kill me." He pleaded. He groveled. "Not ready to die." The gator hung in the water just out of the Lawyer's reach. It watched every movement of the two pieces of meat on the shore. It waited.

The Lawyer leaned down close to the blacksmith's ear. "I'm not going to kill you, asshole." He jerked the blacksmith's head around so he faced the gator. "*That* is."

"Oh, God!" The big man struggled against his bonds. "Oh, God. Mister. Don't. I never killed none of your family. Not one. You can't do this."

"You were there. You watched. You liked watching. As far as I'm concerned, that's the same as cutting or stabbing or shooting."

The gator edged closer, its eyes on the meat standing up and its nose full of fresh blood from the meat lying down. The lawyer grabbed hold of the blacksmith's belt and heaved him closer to the edge. The gator hovered. One more heave and the blacksmith's head touched the water. The gator lunged, jaws lined with three-inch teeth clamped over the blacksmith's shoulder. The gator heaved backward, pulling the screaming blacksmith further into the water. It changed its position, biting deeper into the man's arm. Then it started its death roll. In seconds, the blacksmith's arm was a bloody stump. The gator had ripped it from his body and pulled it from the ropes around the wrists. Blood spurted from torn arteries. The blacksmith's screams said he was no longer human, just prey. The gator struck again, fastening its jaws over the blacksmith's face and neck. The roll started again. This time the gator pulled the meat off the embankment and into the water. Mud bubbled to the top as the gator continued its roll of death down, down, down to the bottom of the bayou.

The Lawyer stood with his hands clasped behind his back, watching the roiling water. Neither blacksmith nor gator came up. Only blood, and mud. The surface of the bayou eventually quieted. The moccasin wiggled back across the water. One more burble of blood rose to the surface. The Lawyer adjusted his wide-brimmed Stetson down over his eyes, then strode to his horse. He coiled the lariat he'd used to drag the blacksmith to the gator's dining table, mounted the blood bay mare, and fastened the lariat to the saddle horn. He patted the Morgan mare on the neck. "That's it, Redemption, Baker was the last of them." He neck-reined the bay around, and took the levee road to the riverboat landing.

* * *

The Hale and Hawkins stage made its usual entrance in a cloud of dust. And as usual, Scarecrow Jim sawed at the reins like the veteran driver he was. But instead of pulling the Concord to a stop in front of the H&H Stage Station, he drove the big coach right on by to Pritchard's Boarding House, a two-story yellow-and-white building at the far end of Main Street.

Two well-dressed men climbed out of the coach. "Driver," shouted the first, a rotund man in his fifties with a leonine shock of white hair. "Driver. I'd be obliged if you'd toss my bags down. Here's a dollar for your trouble." He held a rumpled greenback.

"Shit, Senator Woodruff. I'd toss yer damn trunks down fer nothin', far as that goes." Scarecrow Jim plucked the bill from the fat man's hand anyway.

"And how is it that you know my name?"

"Folks ain't always who they say they is," the driver said. He pulled a newspaper out from under his offside leg and handed it down to Woodruff. The *Cheyenne Gazette's* headline touted, "Senator Woodruff's Plan for Indian Replacement." Beneath the headline, surrounded by type, was an etching of Senator Woodruff himself, the man who now held the newspaper.

The second man out of the coach put on a stovepipe hat as he exited, and he sported a fine hickory cane. He stabbed a finger at the caricature. "No mistake, sir. That's definitely you." Half a smile played on the thin lips of his thin face. "Shouldn't we get inside?" He, too, held up a dollar bill to Scarecrow Jim. "For my baggage, driver."

The driver plucked the bill from the man's hand and started undoing the ropes that held the baggage in place.

"Inside, yes. Well ..." Senator Woodruff glanced up and down Main, which was quiet on that Wednesday night. "I suppose you're right, Mr. Smith."

"Your bags, Senator Woodruff." Scarecrow Jim handed the two heavy leather bags down. Woodruff accepted them one at a time and wrestled them to the boardwalk.

Smith untied his Morgan mare from the rear of the coach, then came back in time to accept his own small bag. The other passengers stayed inside.

Scarecrow Jim cracked his whip above the ears of the lead team and sawed the horse reins, turning the coach around in a broad circle that barely fit the confines of Main Street. A hundred yards down the street, he whipped the teams around again to face the way they'd originally entered town. He whoaed them in front of the H&H station so the other passengers could get out.

Senator Woodruff, obviously not used to carrying his own bags, struggled down the boardwalk toward the front door of the boarding house. Smith led the bay Morgan to the hitching rail, where he looped the reins.

The Morgan immediately went hip-shot as if he'd spent the best years of his life hitched up.

The door opened before Smith and Woodruff reached it. "Good day, senator. I am Anne Pritchard." The woman stood almost as tall as the senator, but had less than half his girth. Her face said she was in her forties, but her hands said she'd lived a hard life. She glanced at Smith, who stood behind Senator Woodruff.

"Pardon me," Woodruff said as he swept a hand toward Smith. "This is J.D. Smith. He did me a favor this evening and I hoped you might provide him with a room."

Anne Pritchard pursed her mouth. "Well, all the rooms are taken, but I can fix up a couch in the den if that is acceptable. Such temporary accommodations are less than room rates, of course."

Smith tipped his tall top hat. "A couch would be more than ample, madam."

"There's a livery about three blocks back down Main."

"Thank you, Mrs. Pritchard, but I'd prefer that Redemption stay close at hand."

"He defecates in front of my boarding house and you'll clean it up, Mr. Smith." The owner of the boarding house didn't seem happy at the idea of Redemption standing in front of her establishment all night.

"Yes, ma'am," Smith said. "May I point out that Redemption is a she, if you please?"

She gave Smith a curt nod. "Come along, senator. Mr. Smith can come after he's tended to his animal friend."

Smith chuckled. He unsaddled the Morgan mare and threw the horse tack over the hitching rail. From the bulging saddlebags, he extracted a gunnysack that had been made into a nosebag. It contained a good quart of oats, and he fitted the bag over Redemption's ears so she could eat while he looked into his accommodations.

* * *

Mrs. Pritchard left Smith in the den and showed Senator Woodruff to his room on the second floor. It proved somewhat larger than the normal hotel room, and it contained a large four-poster, an ornate commode with a china washbasin and water pitcher, two cedar dressers, and luxurious floor-length curtains that set off the carpeted floor.

"Thank you for allowing Mr. Smith the use of the den for the night, Anne," said Senator Woodruff.

Mrs. Pritchard swept across the room to open a curtain. "I do run a boarding house, senator, and extra income in these hard times is always appreciated. Is this Mr. Smith an acquaintance, then?"

"Oh no. We first met on the stage, well, he arrived at the stage at a most fortuitous time."

"Intriguing. Intriguing indeed."

Woodruff poured himself a liberal dollop of bourbon from the complimentary bottle on the nightstand. "Highwaymen assaulted us not long after we left Casper," he said. "Mr. Smith appeared and drove off three of the bandits with the most expertise shooting I have ever seen. He shot two of the men in the shoulder and blew the horse out from under the third. He claims that he abhors killing and shot only to wound. Damnedest thing I ever saw."

"What happened to the outlaws?"

"Smith left them trussed up by the side of the road with a note pinned to the unwounded one proclaiming them outlaws and highwaymen. He said that stretch of road is frequently traveled by lawmen and they would likely be picked up soon. I, of course, invited him to ride in the coach as we were going the same way."

"He seemed quite gentlemanly," Mrs. Pritchard said. "Not at all one who would go in for fancy shooting."

"He shoots extraordinarily well," Woodruff said, stifling a yawn.

"Oh, you must be dead tired. Let me turn down the bedclothes." She went to the four-poster, turned down the covers, and fluffed the pillow. "There. Now, what time do you wish to arise?"

"Six thirty in the morning, if you don't mind. The stage east leaves early, and I must get back to Washington to vote on the Indian bill."

"As you wish, senator."

"Oh, could you also package some victuals for Mr. Smith, compliments of me, please? And I will pay his room fee as well."

"Very good, senator. Would that be all?"

"Yes, it would. Excuse me now, it's been a long day and I'd like to retire."

"Certainly," Mrs. Pritchard said. She swept from the room with her back straight as an iron rod and her skirts swirling.

Senator Woodruff realized he'd kept Scarecrow Jim's newspaper. He sat down in the overstuffed chair near the lamp to read the editorial on his Indian bill. "Lies," he muttered. "Balderdash and lies." He rolled up the paper, smacked his leg with it, and tossed it on the nightstand.

Something tapped at the window.

Woodruff pulled back the curtain to see what. The wind was blowing and the limbs of a big old oak tree brushed the side of the building, making the noise.

Finding the room a bit stuffy, Senator Woodruff decided to open the window. He gave the window frame an upward push. It refused to move. He felt around the frame and found the latch on its top. This he undid, then lifted the window and drank in the warm Cheyenne air.

The senator went back to his overstuffed chair as the breeze ruffled the curtains. He picked up his half-empty glass of bourbon and sipped. A good fragrant whiskey, he found. He picked up the bottle. Old Grand-Dad. Not the most expensive, but excellent as a complimentary bottle. He tipped a bit more into his glass.

He did not even sense the garrote that slipped over his head and drew up tight on his throat. He could not shout for help. He could not breathe. He could not think straight. He struggled to put fingers beneath the cord. He couldn't. The world turned red. He struggled for breath, then struggled for life, kicking and bucking and using the last of his failing strength in trying to escape the cord of death. Thirty long seconds elapsed before Senator Josiah B. Woodruff shuffled off his mortal coil.

His sphincter opened. His bladder voided. He died, his bulging eyes wide open.

* * *

Deputy U.S. Marshal Cash Laramie stepped into the room where Senator Woodruff had been killed, then moved aside as Chief Devon Penn escorted the local doctor toward the exit.

"Thanks, Doc. I'll send someone over for your report later on. And remember," Chief Penn's voice turned hard, "no talking to any newspaper men, or anyone else, for that matter. Don't want rumors getting started, hear?"

The portly doctor shot a glance at Penn's hard face. "Won't, chief. Trust me. Don't like whispering in the dark, and you'll not find rumors starting with me."

"Good, good. Thanks again for coming over." Penn motioned with his hand for the doctor to leave. The medico glanced at Cash as he left, but obviously didn't recognize him. Penn leaned out the door after the doctor left. "Mayo, no one comes in."

"Right, chief," came the reply.

Penn turned to Cash. "A mess, Laramie, a goldam mess."

Cash stepped around the spraddle-legged corpse in the overstuffed chair. "Smells like a goldam mess. Someone did the country a favor. Senator Josiah Woodruff ain't gonna be doing no more voting," he said.

Woodruff's face was bloated. His tongue protruded, stiff and bloody. The eyes stared vacantly into space. Woodruff had not died a pleasant death.

"Hear the senator from Virginia was campaigning to relocate some of our native citizens to lands other than their own," Cash said. He fingered the Arapaho arrowhead he wore on a leather thong around his neck. "Reckon that measure will never pass now."

"But you're not Arapaho." Penn said.

"Naw. All white, whatever that means. Raised by Arapahos, though. Damn good people."

A woman sat in a chair by the window, staring at the floor and wiping tears from her face as they dripped from her eyes. Penn indicated her with a wave of his hand. "This is Mrs. Anne Pritchard, Cash. She found the body. You can get her statement while I take care of the newspaper people. Damn horseflies. Always buzzing around."

"Will do, sir," Cash said.

"Mrs. Pritchard," Penn said.

The woman made no move. She stared at the floor as if she, too, had been garroted to death.

Penn raised his voice. "Mrs. Pritchard!"

She jumped. Her eyelids fluttered. She turned her face toward the chief. "Y–y–es," she managed to say.

"This is Marshal Laramie. He will ask you a few questions, and I'd appreciate it if you gave him full and truthful answers."

The woman blinked, then her back stiffened. "Yes," she said. "Of course."

Penn left the room as Cash grabbed one of the chairs, turned it around and straddled it, arms on the back. "Your statement, ma'am," he said.

The woman said nothing. She just sat there, staring past Cash at the dead body of Josiah Woodruff.

Cash stood, took a blanket from the bed, and covered the corpse. He pulled a tally book and pencil stub from his vest pocket, and sat back down, straddling the chair and balancing the little book on its back. "Statement, Mrs. Pritchard?" he said.

"Thank you, marshal," the woman said.

"Call me Cash, Mrs. Pritchard," he said.

"I'm Anne."

"Tell me what happened. Start when you first saw the senator, please."

Anne Pritchard recounted how the senator and Mr. Smith had arrived, and what had happened when she came to wake the senator early in the morning.

"So you were full up, then, with guests I mean?"

"This is a small guest house, Marshal, er, Cash. Besides the senator and Mr. Smith, there're only two others. Their names are Gramlich and Randall."

Cash nodded. He knew the two men, and figured neither one was a murderer of the kind that would sneak up behind a man and choke him to death with a garrote. That said, Woodruff was a politician, and that meant enemies. In fact, John Wilkes Booth, who shot President Lincoln, was considered an upright citizen before he gunned down the president.

"What about this Mr. Smith?" Cash asked.

Pritchard perked up a little. "Mr. Smith seemed a fine sort," she said. "And he saved the senator during a highwayman holdup of the stage." She repeated the story the senator had told her.

"Do you know where this Smith was headed?"

"He said he was going back to Louisiana."

"Did he say Louisiana was his home?"

"We didn't actually have much of a conversation. He went right to bed, as did I."

"Did he have breakfast?"

"He was gone by the time I went to call the senator at six thirty, so I must assume he didn't eat. And he left his horse tied up outside all night."

"Hmmm. Okay, Anne. That's all. If I think of anything else, I'll look you up."

"Thank you, Cash. I've got cleaning to do, and should be here at the boarding house all day."

"Good. Stick close. The killer may come after you, too. Who knows?"

Anne Pritchard's hand went to her mouth. "Surely—"

"Don't worry. We're around, and Matthew Mayo's a good guard."

Cash watched Anne Pritchard leave the room, appreciating her upright bearing and the graceful sway of her hips. He turned to the window, rereading the notes he'd taken as she talked.

A rap came at the door. "Undertakers," one of the two men standing at the door said. "Come to get a body."

Cash waved at the blanket-covered body, and turned again to the window to read his notes.

"Draw!"

Cash spun to the right as he drew his Colt, earing the hammer back with the web between his fingers and thumb. The undertaker men dropped the body back into the overstuffed chair and took cover behind it. Cash leveled his Colt, but didn't pull the trigger. A slight blond man with a battered Stetson and a modified rifle in a holster against his leg stood crouched with his hand held out, his forefinger pointing like the barrel of a gun.

"Josh Randall!" Cash said, smiling. "Pulling that kind of a trick's gonna get you killed one of these days."

Cash holstered his six-gun, tossed the notebook on the table, and stood up to meet Randall's firm hand-shake. "How the hell are you, bounty hunter?"

"Well as can be expected, Cash. Doing fine." He looked at Cash and his eyes turned the color of hard blue agates. "You know, Cash. I saw something last night that you just might be interested in. Let me tell you about it."

* * *

"Cash, this telegram don't mean nothing."

"Lemme see." Cash reached over the counter and snatched the yellow paper from the telegraph operator's hand. "It's just Miles' gibberish," he said. He put a dime on the counter. "Get yourself a sarsaparilla, Marcus. I can read his message."

Cash Laramie and Gideon Miles, Deputy U.S. Marshals both, often exchanged telegrams in code. This was one of the simpler ones. The codes were not meant to stand up to close scrutiny, but they served to keep casual readers from understanding the contents. Helped stave off gossip. Cash picked out his friend's message from the clutter of redundant words and words spelled backward.

THE LAWYER IS WORKING IN CHEYENNE.

* * *

Penn read the message twice, the real words written by Cash below the code. "So you think the man in the stovepipe hat, that Mr. Smith, you think he killed the senator?"

"Not ready to bet my whole hand on it, but I'd like to find him and ask him a question or two. Up close and personal." Cash smoothed the rim of his Stetson and put it back on his head. "You know, I kinda thought all that talk about The Lawyer was a story, but like some other stories you hear, there's a lot of fact mixed in with the fantasy. Killer all right. But not just one. No one man could do all the slaying he has been accused of. My reckoning anyway."

"Could be. Those dime novels don't help either. But we've cleaned up before, we can do it again." Penn leaned back. His chair creaked under his weight. "You've got an idea where the stovepipe man is, then?"

Cash handed over another telegram. "I've got a gambler friend who says he played with Smith at the

Black Mask in Wounded Dove. I'd like to go over and play a hand, see what I can dig up."

"He the same one that saw him at Pritchard's boarding house?"

"No, that was Josh Randall. Charlie Gramlich— he's a gambler and sometimes hired gun—he's now in Wounded Dove. From where I stand, his word's as good or better than that of any lawman in the territory."

Penn leaned forward, and the chair complained again. "My secretary will give you some traveling money. You'll have to sign for it and you'll have to bring back what you don't use."

"How many times do you think I've done this, Boss?" Cash's smile took the sting from his words.

"Man forgets," Penn said. "Wire me when you know something. Newspapers are bloodhounding. Washington wants results."

Cash set his black Stetson low on his forehead. He put a finger to its brim. "Yes, sir."

* * *

Wounded Dove, Wyoming had the world by the tail with a downhill pull. Men knew they could go to its saloons for friendly card games, a little bucking the tiger, and for warm friendly conversation and other things from the doves who worked the floors. Its general store held the supplies people needed. Wyoming ranches were thriving. The winter had been mild, and Wounded Dove the town was reaping the rewards. New people came every day, and a gaggle of pumpkin rollers had taken out claims on land watered by Rock Creek to the south. Growth. That was the name of the game. Growth.

Cash Laramie recognized the town though he'd never been here before. It was the same as other new towns in the territory—lusty, energetic, loose in some ways, hard and tough in others. It was the kind of town that made a country grow. A little wild, maybe, but full of vitality. He pulled Paint to a stop in front of the Black Mask saloon, dismounted and looped the reins over the hitching rail. He slapped the dust from his clothing, then unpinned his badge and slipped it in a vest pocket. Putting a hand on each side of the batwing doors, he pushed them open.

The room, like the town, was familiar. Bar down the left-hand side of the room. Tables down the right. Desultory card game going on at the far table. None of the players was Charlie Gramlich and none matched the description of Mr. Smith. Cash moved to the bar, and the barman behind it moved to meet him.

The barkeep swiped at the bar top with a damp towel. "What'll ya have, sor?"

Cash looked closer. "Ronald O'Hara? Is that you, man?"

"Aye, but it is, sor. Are ye still toting a badge, sor?"

Cash lowered his voice. "Not so's you'd notice, Ronald. Not so's you'd notice." He winked. "Tell me. Charlie Gramlich been around?"

O'Hara swiped the bar with the towel again and leaned closer to Cash. "Charlie's been here all right, Cash. Been and gone. Dunno why he left in such a hurry, but he did. Done and gone, he is."

"What're the poker stakes like?"

"Right now, penny ante. Ain't nobody over there who rolls on the high end."

"Ya got Maryland Rye?"

"Have we got Maryland Rye? Is Hell hot? Do angels have wings? Bet your bottom cookie we've got Maryland Rye. Why?"

"I'll have a bottle."

"Sor, that's a sissy drink, it is. Have something with body, like Jameson's."

Cash shook his head and smiled. "Know where you're coming from, O'Hara, but I've got to keep my head on my shoulders. Can't afford to get tipsy."

"If you say so, sor." O'Hara went to get the drink.

Cash took the opportunity to watch the card game. The players looked like ranchers, except for the house gambler, a man in a white shirt with garters on the sleeves.

"Yer rye, sor," O'Hara said.

"Thanks. How much?"

"Two bits, Cash, sor."

Cash laughed. "Always preferred that," he said. "That's how I got my name." He paid, took the bottle by the neck, and wandered over to watch the card game.

When one of the ranchers pulled out, Cash said, "Gentlemen. Mind if I sit in?"

The card players swept him with hard glances, measuring him as an opponent. All they saw was a trail-worn rider with dust on his hat, black shirt, vest, and trousers, all dusty, and black boots that had seen better days. Cash's Arapaho arrowhead and its leather thong hid beneath his shirt.

"Help yourself," the oldest rancher said.

Cash sat down and put his bottle on the table. "Five card stud?" he said.

"You got it," the old rancher said. "Nickel ante."

"Fine with me." Cash would be paying with expense money from Penn's secretary, but he didn't worry about it. He won more often than he lost at poker tables.

Over a slow half hour, Cash managed to lose three times out of four. *Not my money.* The men were not good poker players and kept their stakes low. No wonder Gramlich had moved on. He did find out that a man called J.D. Smith usually came in to gamble in late afternoon, often staying until dawn, if there was any action.

"Seems a nice chap," a rancher said. "Plays for the fun of the game. Never seen him upset over a hand, his or another's."

"Reckon he'll be in today, then?" Cash asked, looking at his cards with a serious expression. "Might he play for a little more than nickel ante?"

"Dunno" was the dealer's answer.

The game went on. The mousy looking girl who served drinks lit the coal-oil lamps. "Hey, Mona," a man at the far table hollered. "Gimme another whiskey, would ya?"

"Hold your damn horses, cowboy. Can't you see I'm lighting the lamps?" She laughed, as a floor woman should. Never pays to rile a customer. Cash watched her.

"Hey, mister. We got a card game going here. Wanna watch the butts and tits, go back to the bar." The rancher who spoke was a steady loser, but didn't seem to worry about it. He seemed to enjoy the bluff and counter bluff.

About the time Mona finished lighting the lamps, J.D. Smith walked in. He took a moment to note the position of everyone in the saloon. His eyes stopped at the card table. Two of the ranchers who'd been playing poker had already left, so Cash, the gambler whose name was Henry, and a rancher named Franks were the only ones at the card table.

Smith ordered a whiskey from Mona, removed his stovepipe, and came over to the poker table. "Mind?" he asked.

Cash shrugged. Franks nodded. Henry indicated an empty chair. "Five card stud," he said. "Nickel stakes."

"Thank you." Smith sat. "Gentlemen," he said. "Shall we begin?"

Henry held up the deck, and O'Hara came with a new one.

Cash sized Smith up, without seeming to watch him. Height: five eight. Weight: a hundred fifty pounds or so. Late thirties. Seemed a bit of a dandy, but also had an electric aura of danger that showed from deep within his black eyes.

Smith sipped his whiskey, a slight smile on his face. He kept his eyes straight ahead, looking at a place somewhere between Cash and the bar. Cash knew

Smith was watching with peripheral vision. This was a man to steer clear of.

After the third hand, Smith beckoned Mona over. "Could you get me a plate of that good roast beef from the Garvey Hotel restaurant? Baked potato, too. Lots of gravy. Hmm?"

"Yes, sir, Mr. Smith. Right away." Mona hustled out the batwings and around to the restaurant, which was next door to the saloon.

Cash won the next hand. He left his winnings on the table in front of his chair and stood. "Henry, I'm gonna stretch my legs and have a cigar. When I get back, I'd like to play another round. Okay?"

"You got it," the gambler said.

Cash seemingly paid no attention to Smith, but he felt the man's deadly eyes following him as he left the saloon. He reached into an inner pocket of his vest and withdrew a cheroot. He paused a moment, hunching his shoulders to shield the cheroot as he lit it with a lucifer scratched against the saloon wall. He ambled past the window behind the card table and continued down to the telegraph office on Commerce Street. There was no reply to the wire he'd sent earlier. He returned to the game.

Smith was still eating his meal, but when he finished, he came back to play with Cash, Henry the gambler, and a wealthy rancher named Harlow Wilson. Franks had left as soon as the stakes went up. Before long, raises were a minimum of five dollars, then ten. News of the big money game flew around Cheyenne and people gathered to watch the card players. Wilson dropped out, for all his claims of wealth from a ranch in Arizona, another in Texas, and a beginning in Wyoming. Henry dealt. Smith and Cash played.

"What's that I see around your neck, sir?" Smith asked. "An arrowhead? Unusual to say the least."

"Won it in a poker game," Cash said. "Dodge City."

"Is that right? Earp still the tin star there?"

Cash sipped at his Maryland. "Last I heard, Dodge was under the thumb of a man named Dillon. Matt Dillon. Big tall sucker."

"Dillon? Never heard of him."

Henry dealt the cards. Smith picked up his and fanned them out for a look. He rubbed the bridge of his nose, his eyes calculating.

Cash got an ace and some garbage. He decided to talk. "If you don't mind my asking, where you from?"

"Don't mind at all," Smith said. He tossed a card and Henry gave him a new one. "Rayne, Louisiana," he said.

"You're a long way from home, mister ..." Cash fished for a name.

"Smith. J.D. Smith. I travel around on business."

Came time to put up or shut up and Cash folded, losing more of Penn's money.

"What about you? Don't believe I got your name."

"West. James West," Cash said. "I do some of this and some of that. Up here because I heard there's mining interests coming in, and that interests me."

"Mining interest, shit," said an onlooker. "Only ones making money from mining interests is them with money. Them's the ones bringing in chinks 'cause they work cheaper than micks or spades. Mining interests, my ass."

The argument spread and the noise level in the saloon went up three levels. Good thing a man doesn't think with his ears. Cash signaled for a card to replace the one he discarded. Henry dealt it with a deadpan face. Smith acted as if they were playing cards on some distant shore with no more than the lap-swish of waves to disrupt the silence.

"Mining, Mr. West," Smith said. "That could be quite risky. Would you be accustomed to taking big risks?"

"Done it a time or two," Cash said. "Raise you ten." He shoved a chip into the middle of the table.

"You really shouldn't do that, West. This will make the fourth hand you've lost in the last hour, and your pile of chips looks rather thin." Smith showed a whisper of a smile, but didn't look at Cash as he spoke.

"I'll damn well play cards the way I want to play them," Cash said, his voice a little louder than necessary. Talk of mining lapsed and the onlookers turned their attention to the game once more.

Smith's little smile remained. His black eyes were flat, expressionless, deadly. On the table before him lay one card face down, a jack of spades, a jack of diamonds, and a deuce of clubs. On the surface, Cash had the advantage with two queens and a ten of spades.

"Check," Smith said. Henry dealt two more cards, an eight of hearts to Smith, a four of clubs to Cash.

Smith's bet.

"Well, West. It comes down to the hole card, does it not?" Smith rubbed the bridge of his nose with a forefinger. "Ten," he said, shoving a chip to the center of the table.

Cash pasted a matching little smile on his own face. "Match ten, raise ten." His blue eyes bore into Smith's.

Smith nodded. "Call."

Cash flipped over his hidden card. A queen of diamonds. "That gives me three of a kind," he said. "No way you can top that."

Smith nodded again. "Almighty lucky all of a sudden," he said.

"Gotta win once in a while. You've been mowing 'em down all evening. How'd you work it so's I'd win, sharpy?"

Smith eyed Cash with quiet distain. "Are you saying I cheated, West?"

Cash fastened Smith with smoky eyes. He reached across to the empty chair where Smith had deposited his stovepipe hat. Calmly he placed his palm on the top and squashed it flat. "If the hat fits, Smith, wear it."

Smith stood smoothly, his eyes never leaving Cash's face. He stepped back from the chairs surrounding the table to a clear space, then took a ready stance. His hand hovered over the walnut handles of a Remington Army .45. Spectators cleared out from behind him.

"How do you want to call this one, West? You can only insult a Southern gentleman so far, you know."

Cash kept the thin smile on his face. His blue eyes harkened back to the sundance trial of his youth. His face could have been hacked from granite. He opened his mouth, but the double-click of shotgun hammers being eared back cut him short.

"Alright," the bartender said. "No shooting my place up. Understood?"

Cash let his body relax. He retrieved his Stetson and placed it low over his brow. He smiled the thin smile at Smith. "Never you mind, Ronald. Mr. Smith and I will settle our differences elsewhere. Is that not correct, Smith?"

"We will do that, West. We surely will."

"I'll take my money, Henry."

"Will do." The gambler counted out bills for Cash's chips. Not as much of Penn's money as he'd laid down, but a decent repay.

"Later then, Smith." Cash touched a finger to the brim of his hat in salute.

"Yes, West. Later." Smith sat back down.

Cash left the saloon, not worrying about a back-shot from Smith or anyone else. And they would have been surprised to see the broad smile on his face.

* * *

On his way out of town, Cash stopped by the telegraph office so the sun was long down by the time he got to Snooker Ridge. Cash tied Paint off the trail and out of sight, then took cover in a jumble of boulders. He heard the clip-clop of Smith's walking horse minutes before it came abreast of his hiding place. He could tell The Lawyer was in no hurry.

Just before he passed Cash, Smith spoke. "That you, Laramie?"

"It is. Just keep your hands on the saddle horn and we'll be just fine."

"An execution? Not like a marshal, I'd say." Smith's voice carried a hint of irony, but there was no tremble of fear in it.

"Thought we could palaver a bit," Cash said.

"We could've talked at the card table."

"How'd you figure out who I am?"

"Arrowhead. Heard of a U.S. Marshal named Cash Laramie who always wore one. Besides, James West hasn't been around these parts for years. The Secret Service only scouts the way when the president heads in this direction."

"James West's a pretty common name."

"But you're not a common-appearing man. So. What do you want?"

"Why the stovepipe. That went out with Lincoln."

"Haberdasher friend made it for me. What of it?"

"Josh Randall saw you making a quick exit from Anne Pritchard's boarding house. And I've got a copy of the telegram you sent to Washington. It says, 'JOB FINISHED STOP MAKE FINAL PAYMENT.' Reckon the money's why you're still in these parts."

Smith said nothing for a long moment. Then, "Is that all, Laramie? Nothing you've got'll stand up in a court of law, you know."

"The Lawyer, eh? Why would a defender like you start killing?"

"None of your concern, Laramie. None at all. I'm going to start my horse down the trail. If you shoot, you'll shoot me in the back."

"Whoa. Who said anything about back-shooting? Besides, sometimes killing is more than justified. A rich kid shot my friend in cold blood, just because he was Arapaho. I killed him. It was a gunfight, but I killed him."

Smith heaved a sigh. "So what."

"So a bunch of rowdies fired up on bad whiskey and worse opium raped your Cheyenne wife, then killed her and your children, hacking them up in a frenzy, leaving their bodies scattered all over your house. Right?"

The Lawyer's shoulders hunched as if he were enduring incredible pain. Words hissed from his clenched jaw. "None. Of. Your. Fucking. Business, tin star."

Cash released the hammer of his Colt and returned it to its holster. He stepped out of the jumble of rocks and walked up alongside The Lawyer. "Smith, I'm not trying to egg you. I know exactly where you're coming from. Those hard cases that did your family in, they died. I know they died. I have no proof, but if I'd been you, they'd die. And I reckon that's what put you on the side of justice."

"Justice. What the hell is justice, Laramie?" The depth of The Lawyer's pain was mirrored in his words.

"I know you kill for hire, Smith. I also hear that you never kill just for the money. I hear there's got to be a miscarriage of justice involved."

"How do you figure that? You as much as accused me of killing Senator Woodruff, whose life I saved from a bunch of stagecoach robbers."

"But you didn't kill those owlhoots. You left them wounded for me or another lawman to find."

"Well. Yeah. They weren't nothing to me. Who knows? They might go straight after some time in jail."

"See? Justice. So there's got to be some justice involved in the Woodruff killing."

"The people he's moving off their land are relatives of my wife."

"And the senator's vote was the deciding one," Cash said. "But I'd sure be interested in knowing who paid you to do it, but I don't reckon there's any kind of a trail I could follow to the source of that money." He paid no more attention to Smith while he walked back to Paint, untied him, and mounted. When he reached the trail, Smith was waiting, his Remington in his hand.

"Sometime you may trust the wrong man, Laramie." The Lawyer said. He leveled the six-gun at Cash.

Cash grinned and adjusted the black Stetson on his head. He turned his back and kneed Paint on down the trail. But the horse had only taken two steps when The Lawyer's Remington crashed. A pine bough, snipped from an overhanging limb, dropped on Cash's shoulder. He reined Paint to a stop.

"Sometime you may trust the wrong man, Laramie," The Lawyer repeated. "But this time, trusting my honor served you well." Smith holstered his Remington.

Cash pulled a cheroot from his vest and bit off its end. He rolled it into the corner of his mouth without lighting it. "Pay you to stay out of my neck of the woods, lawyer man."

The Lawyer removed his stovepipe and smoothed it into its proper shape. "Done," he said. "Good day, Marshal Laramie."

†

Other titles from BEAT to a PULP

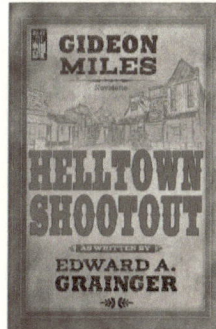
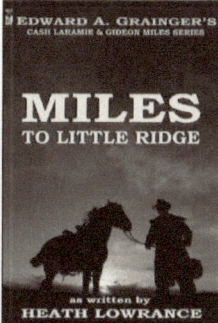
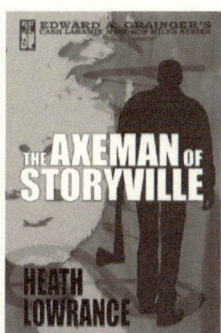

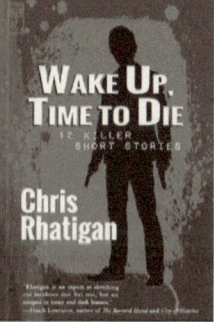

 BEAT to a PULP
PO Box 173
Freeville, New York 13068
USA
Email: btapzine@beattoapulp.com
Visit us at www.beattoapulp.com